"There's a pure wildcat under your pretty pink skin, Madam Mayor," Rucker taunted in a wicked, throaty voice.

"Temporary insanity. I've never—"

"Acted so un-mayorly . . . before," he finished for her. "I know." His voice dropped to a low murmur against her ear. "But, oh, little lady, you're gonna surprise yourself a whole lot more than this before I'm through."

He curved his hands around her waist and abruptly picked her up. Dinah gripped his shoulders as he pulled her close and held her snugly to him. He was a big man, and she trembled at the sensation of being overwhelmed.

"All right?" he asked.

"I'm just feeling particularly female at the moment." She didn't tell him that this dignified and pristine female had no idea how to deal with a man who ruffled her reserve . . . and everything else.

"I'll take that as a compliment," he said in an amused tone.

"It is, macho man, it is."

"You Jane, me Tarzan."

"You Rambo, me . . . I don't know who I am." She sounded resigned.

"You're a prim little ol' beauty queen who's come to her senses. You need to run wild a little." She moaned as he pressed his body closer to her. "Come on, Dee. Run wild with me. . . ."

WHAT ARE *LOVESWEPT* ROMANCES?

They are stories of true romance and touching emotion. We believe those two very important ingredients are constants in our highly sensual and very believable stories in the *LOVESWEPT* line. Our goal is to give you, the reader, stories of consistently high quality that may sometimes make you laugh, sometimes make you cry, but are always fresh and creative and contain many delightful surprises within their pages.

Most romance fans read an enormous number of books. Those they truly love, they keep. Others may be traded with friends and soon forgotten. We hope that each *LOVESWEPT* romance will be a treasure—a "keeper." We will always try to publish

LOVE STORIES YOU'LL NEVER FORGET
BY AUTHORS YOU'LL ALWAYS REMEMBER

The Editors

LOVESWEPT® • 255

Deborah Smith
Hold On Tight

BANTAM BOOKS
TORONTO • NEW YORK • LONDON • SYDNEY • AUCKLAND

This is for Myra and Don—sophisticated, glamorous, and two of the most loving people I know. They continue to provide me with worlds of romantic inspiration.

HOLD ON TIGHT

A Bantam Book / May 1988

LOVESWEPT® and the wave device are registered trademarks of Bantam Books. Registered in U.S. Patent and Trademark Office and elsewhere.

If you would be interested in receiving protective vinyl covers for your Loveswept books, please write to this address for information:

Loveswept
Bantam Books
P.O. Box 985
Hicksville, NY 11802

ISBN 0-553-21894-8

Published simultaneously in the United States and Canada

Bantam Books are published by Bantam Books, a division of Bantam Doubleday Dell Publishing Group, Inc. Its trademark, consisting of the words "Bantam Books" and the portrayal of a rooster, is Registered in U.S. Patent and Trademark Office and in other countries. Marca Registrada. Bantam Books, 666 Fifth Avenue, New York, New York 10103.

PRINTED IN THE UNITED STATES OF AMERICA

O   0 9 8 7 6 5 4 3 2 1

One

"Boss, I have a baby possum for you."

"Miss Hunstomper, I distinctly recollect telling you that I wanted fried chicken and cole slaw for lunch, not baby possum."

"This is no joke, boss. Now look, that Alabama mayor you wrote the column about—the ex-Miss Georgia—has taken revenge. I guess it's because you called her a 'possum queen' and made fun of her town's Possum Days Festival."

Rucker McClure finished double-checking his latest column and slowly lowered the Lifestyle section of *The Birmingham Herald/Examiner*. When the top edge of the paper was just beneath the level of his eyes, he arched one auburn brow at his secretary. Nothing about his handsome face indicated that he believed her claim that a baby possum was now residing on the editorial floor of one of the South's largest daily newspapers.

"A possum, you say, Miss Hunstomper?"

His feet, encased in custom-made eel-skin cowboy boots—a hint that his taxable income had been half a million dollars last year—remained nonchalantly cushioned on top of a golf bag, and the golf bag remained stretched out like a beached whale across one end of his crowded desk.

"Miss Hunstomper," he drawled in a deep voice as mellow as ripe peaches, "after three years of bein' overpaid to do whatever it is you do here, you ought to recognize how important I am and stop tryin' to drive me crazy."

She exhaled in disgust. Rucker grinned affectionately as the pretty, businesslike blonde kept her truant stance in his doorway. The sixth-floor newsroom stretched out behind her as a reminder that the rest of the world was a serious place. As usual, Millie Surprise—known to Rucker's readers as Miss Hunstomper—finally grinned back at him. "I'm not joking, Your Majesty. There's a live possum out here on my desk, in a wire cage. A courier just left it for you."

"You're serious."

"You bet."

"Good grief." An incredulous smile crept across his face. "Bring my gift critter on in here," he ordered cheerfully.

Millie gingerly set the wire cage in the middle of his desk. Rucker made room by pushing aside a stack of *Sports Illustrated* magazines, his baseball autographed by the Atlanta Braves, and the keys to his Cadillac. Then he opened the cage door.

"It looks like a giant rat! It might bite!" Millie exclaimed. "It might be rabid!"

"Naaah. Millie, where I grew up in south Texas, the only pets we could afford were possums. We'd peel 'em off the road—"

"Oh, please. Save the lurid details for a column."

Chuckling, Rucker reached inside the cage and tickled the small gray animal under its long snout. At about the size of a half-grown kitten, the possum didn't look threatening. It peered up at him with beady, timid eyes. He slid one hand under it and lifted it out, then cradled it to his stomach. Its long, hairless tail curled around Rucker's wrist in a frightened way.

"Poor baby," Rucker crooned gently. "Millie, gimme that letter from Madam Mayor, the possum queen."

She handed him a sheet stamped with the official seal of Mount Pleasant, Alabama. "Seat of Twittle County," Rucker read in a wry tone. "That's one of the few backwoods places I've never heard of, and I thought I'd swilled beer and chased women everywhere south of the Mason-Dixon line." He scanned the letter quickly, smiling all the time. "Listen to what Madam Mayor says, Millie. 'Mr. McClure, if you are ever again so desperate for material that you besmirch the good name and good people of Mount Pleasant, I shall personally supervise the shipment of a second opposum to your office. Along with it, you will receive notice of a libel suit.' "

Rucker put the letter down, his eyes gleaming with intrigue. "For an ex-beauty queen, she sounds pretty smart," he commented.

"One of the reporters looked up an old article about her after your column ran. Just for curiosity. She has a Mensa-level IQ, boss," Millie informed him. "And a master's degree in political science. She probably would have been Miss America six years ago, if she hadn't walked out a day before the competition. Her father had died a month earlier in an airplane crash. She said the pageant didn't matter anymore."

"Sounds like a gutsy woman."

"You better leave her alone. She's not your type—she can read, write, and think. You swore you'd never have anything to do with that kind of woman again, remember?"

"That was personal, m' dear. This is professional." Rucker leaned back in his chair. The possum crawled up his shirt and buried its dark little nose in the soft chest hair above his unbuttoned collar. Rucker stroked its back and nodded to himself, thinking. "Call Mount Pleasant and find out when the next city-council meetin' is. I'm goin' to visit Madam Mayor."

After a stunned second, Millie said with glee, "Trouble. We got trouble my friends, right here in Possum City."

Dinah Sheridan hummed a little—a section from the Mozart piece she'd practiced on her piano before breakfast that morning—as she studied paperwork and made notes for the September city-council meeting. As usual she was efficient. Also as usual she was dressed tastefully, and her long, chocolate-colored hair was bundled in a perfect twist at the base of her neck. Her business-like demeanor belied the fact that the body under her outfit had stolen many a judge's breath in swimsuit competitions. She sighed with contentment and smoothed a hand over the blue unstructured jacket she wore with a colorful sweater and neat gray skirt.

Outside the small windows that lined one wall of the council room, a cool Monday night had already closed in on the mountains around tiny Mount Pleasant, population 4,231. Inside, harsh fluorescent light-bulbs cast white streaks on the cheap-paneled walls.

"Dinah, you shame the rest of us to death by gettin' here so early," Walter Higgins joked as he ambled into the room. He sat down beside her at the long council platform, a wide V built of darkly stained plywood.

"We've got a big agenda tonight," Dinah told the white-haired building contractor, a former mayor himself.

"Did you ever hear from Rucker McClure?"

"No. He got the oppossum—the possum—and the letter last Thursday. I suppose I terrified him."

"That old boy doesn't terrify easy. He's an important sonuvagun, you know. That column of his goes to newspapers all over the country. And he was on that dirty cable show, you know. Talkin' to that Dr. Ruth woman." Walter chuckled. "He told her his favorite sex toy is white bread and mayonnaise."

"I've never seen him, and I don't ever care to. He's an overgrown adolescent. I don't care if his last book did make *The New York Times*'s bestseller list. *True Grits.* What a precocious little title." Dinah made an elegantly derisive sound that dismissed Rucker McClure and his redneck schtick. "He's trying to compete with Lewis Grizzard."

"It was a real funny book," Walter countered. "People are sayin' Rucker McClure is the modern-day Mark Twain."

"Bite your tongue," Dinah said wryly. "That's sacrilege."

The other council members strolled in: Fred Dawson, Jasper Mac Seagram, and Glory Akens. They were respected, local business people and amiable friends of

Dinah's. Following them, rocking along on short, plump legs, was placid Lula Belle Mitchum, a graying brunette who had been city clerk of Mount Pleasant for the past twenty years. Politicians come and go, Dinah thought, but Lula Belle endures.

Within thirty minutes half the council chamber's fifty audience chairs had been filled by townsfolk. The police chief sat in a corner yawning, waiting to make his monthly report. The fire chief and the city attorney were finishing a game of checkers on a table by the water fountain in the hall.

Dinah cleared her throat, rapped her gavel, and smiled at the audience. People smiled back as she called the meeting to order, and Dinah's chest swelled with satisfaction. She'd left a lot of trouble and sorrow behind when she arrived here four years ago. Her smile widened. "First on our agenda tonight is a zoning variance for Pop's Seed and Feed . . ."

Things went smoothly for the next forty-five minutes as one item after another passed under her gavel. She was authoritative without being rude, and people respected her opinions.

Dinah sat with her head down, making a note on the pad by her right hand. As she listened to Fred discuss the Founder's Day Dinner Dance, she stifled a yawn and raised her head to idly study the audience.

The unexpected newcomer sat in the front row barely three feet away, looking back at her—no, staring back at her. Dinah glanced down, blinked several times as if to test the accuracy of her vision, then looked back up. Tall—he was over six feet tall. She could estimate that, even though he was sitting down, one booted foot propped on the opposite denimed knee.

He nodded to her slightly, his head tilted to one side, his expression very intense, and his eyes riveted to her face. Dinah caught her breath then nodded back to him. All very polite, she thought. If only her pulse would slow to a polite gallop. She looked down, frowned in serious concentration, and drew some doodles on her note pad. She glanced back up casually, her demeanor very formal, very Katharine Hepburn, she thought, patting her hair.

He caught her attention again with one devilishly lifted eyebrow, a simple gesture, really, but appealing and funny. Dinah looked back down at her pad. Fred was still talking, and she pretended to make a note.

"Overconfident, oversexed," she wrote, then scratched it out so that no one would think she meant Fred. The stranger seemed unusually sure of himself, and that intrigued her as much as it unsettled her. Most men weren't confident, not around a former Miss Georgia who happened to have a high IQ and a forthright attitude.

Dinah looked up frowning and stared straight at him. He gazed back so intensely that she couldn't look away. Few other men would have been so attractive in jeans, a nondescript houndstooth jacket, and a shirt with wide plaid stripes. Those jeans, oh, dear. If a man wore loose, new jeans with ornamental stitching on the outside, he was fairly tame, probably a little shy, and mostly dependable. But if a man wore snug, faded jeans, he was asking the world to notice that all the ornaments were on the inside, and womankind had best beware. This stranger wore those kind of jeans.

She swept an admiring gaze over his thick auburn hair and mustache. He had a terrific face, she decided, a well-lived-in face with a lot of kindness tucked into the laugh lines. His mouth curved into a vague smile in response to her attention. He looked as stunned as she felt, Dinah realized suddenly. Then he winked, and she knew that her scrutiny was being analyzed, appreciated, and returned. He knew she was leering.

". . . and so, Madam Mayor, I propose that we charge seven-fifty a head for the dance," Fred concluded. "Your opinion?"

Dinah jerked her eyes away from the provocative auburn-haired stranger and stared at Fred. Fred stared back. "Well?" he asked patiently. "What do you think?"

"I . . . think . . ." Dinah had no idea what he'd just said. Self-rebuke shot through her. She was a serious woman, a serious mayor. It wasn't like her to be so air brained. "I . . . think . . ." She turned to Glory, a be-spectacled grandmother who owned the local bakery. "What do you think?" Dinah asked her.

Glory eyed her askance for a moment, then took up the slack and began talking. Dinah cautiously let her gaze drift back to the disturbing stranger. He was grinning, nearly laughing, his green eyes crinkled deeply at the corners. He knew exactly what he'd done to her concentration. Dinah bit her lip and glared at him. He tugged his mouth downward and looked absurdly chastised.

An awful thing happened to her. Her mouth tingled with a rebellious urge to smile. Amazed, Dinah let her lips part in temptation. Underneath all the teasing in his eyes was something corny and sweet, something that made her think of country mornings, church bells on Sunday, dancing by firelight with the kids in bed upstairs and the dog asleep on the couch. . . .

Something was crawling up his back. Dinah barely contained her gasp as a small pink paw reached over his shoulder and grasped the lapel of his sport coat. Her hand jumped in shock, upsetting an empty coffee cup next to her notepad. The cup rolled over and she fumbled with it, her eyes never leaving the paw. The stranger's eyebrows shot up as he felt something pulling on his jacket, but his movements were calm as he turned his head. Dinah noticed suddenly that everyone behind him was in quiet hysterics, their faces red with restrained laughter.

A small possum climbed sluggishly atop the stranger's broad shoulder, then sat there sniffing the air. Dinah felt all the blood leave her face as she noticed that it wore a slender black collar and leash. This assertive possum had not wandered in by himself, then.

The stranger gauged her puzzled reaction then raised one hand and showed her that he held the end of the possum's leash. He gave her a jaunty guess-who look, and she felt her eyes widening in startled recognition. Only one man would have reason to deliberately bring a possum into her council meeting. Rucker McClure.

No. Oh, no. What had she wrought with her stern

letter and possum ploy? She hadn't terrified Rucker McClure at all, she'd provoked him. She'd provoked a nationally syndicated columnist known for down-home humor and scalding truth. If he had come here to search out the truth about her, she'd be ruined.

Dinah rapped her gavel, her hand shaking. Glory stopped talking. "Excuse me, Mrs. Akens," Dinah said firmly, "but we seem to have a disturbance in the audience." She pointed the gavel at Rucker McClure. "Do you have business here tonight, sir?"

He straightened and uncrossed his legs. The possum was unsettled by the movement and nearly toppled over. Rucker reached up with one big hand and caught it gently. It squeaked, then climbed with amazing speed to the top of his head, where it perched happily. People gasped. After a breathless moment of silence the fire chief, Frank Raffer, spoke in a strained voice.

"If my wife sees that hat, she'll want one just like it." Frank went into a convulsive hee-hee-hee-hee. Order collapsed. Anna Jenkins, a pert little old lady, nearly fell out of her chair laughing. Ten-year-old Clyde Daniels giggled so hard that he dropped his Ninja star. The city attorney, Mac Windham, guffawed and held his stomach. Dinah propped her chin on one hand and squinted at Rucker McClure as if she'd like to choke him.

"Madam Mayor, I apologize," he said, giving her a surprisingly earnest look. After the hysterics died to a reasonable level, he stood up, pulled the possum off his head, and cradled it in one hand. "In case anybody here hasn't figured it out yet, I'm Rucker McClure, that redneck sonuvagun who makes more money than he's worth writin' for *The Birmingham Herald/Examiner.* Your mayor has taken exception to a little column I wrote about a week ago."

His voice was incredibly deep and smooth, like warm cognac, Dinah thought. It was very persuasive and it overflowed with a melodic southern accent. "I suppose I owe you a rebuttal, Mr. McClure," she allowed stiffly. "You have five minutes."

He bowed, a southern gentleman in a badly coordinated shirt and jacket, Rhett Butler with no fashion sense—yet totally intriguing. "I've come to admit my fault and say I never meant any harm by pickin' on y'all a little," he soothed. He turned to face the audience better. The man's a natural orator, Dinah recalled someone saying. She could believe it. His charm had captured the council, the audience, and her imagination.

"I'm reminded of a story," he began happily. People perched on the edges of their chairs, wiping laughter from their eyes and listening. "When I was a little ol' boy growin' up in Multree, Texas, where the women aren't nearly as pretty as they are here"—he glanced coyly back at Dinah—"why, in high school, Veda Jane Veegle, my first true love, was voted Most Likely to Become a Marine. But back to my story . . ."

Seated on the yellow vinyl of a booth at the Lucky Duck Diner sipping coffee, Dinah kept a pleasant expression on her face and listened with forced politeness as the other council members bombarded Rucker McClure with questions about his writing and the celebrities he'd met. She'd decided to be nice to him and hustle him out of town in a congenial mood.

Rucker answered distractedly, his scrambled emotions hidden under the usual good-old-boy routine. The cool beauty across the table was the living picture of his best daydreams. She was regal, tall, and sturdy —no frail flower of southern womanhood, that was for sure—and he wanted to keep looking at her forever. Some of her features were classic—a wide, perfect smile between slender lips, a small, tilted nose, a clear, silk-smooth complexion—but others were decidedly unusual by beauty queen standards.

Her jaw was strong and her eyes, whew, her eyes were stunning. A light china blue, surrounded by dark brunette lashes that matched her hair, they stood out like twin beacons. Intelligence and confidence radiated from those serious eyes, and the combination was extremely sexy, whether she intended it to be or not. Every time he looked away from her he knew that she studied him with unwavering intensity. The air between them seemed warm, and not from the steam off their coffee.

"Well, I gotta go," Glory Akens said, yawning. "It's ten-thirty. Thanks for the coffee and pie, Mr. McClure—I mean, Rucker. That's apology enough for me."

"Me too," echoed Jasper Mac, running a hand over his hairless head. "It was good meetin' you."

He and Glory got up from the booth. Walter and Fred, seated in chairs at the end, stood also and said their good nights. Dinah started to get up, too, but Rucker casually put a hand across the table and touched her arm. "Let's you and me talk awhile, Mayor. I'll give you a ride back to city hall."

Dinah looked into his eyes and saw serious invitation. Her heart rate would never be normal again after tonight, she was certain. This man didn't even attempt to act subtle. Worse yet, before she'd learned who he was, she hadn't concealed her interest. She was trapped.

"I rode with Jasper Mac," she said. "It's not polite—"

"Oh, shoot, Dinah, you know I don't mind," Jasper Mac interjected.

Dinah sighed. Trapped. Well, she'd spent years on the beauty pageant circuit, and she was an expert at derailing onrushing men. She could certainly sidetrack this celebrity Romeo. "All right," she answered.

She trailed a wistful gaze after her friends and allies as they went out into the cool night. Now it was just her, Rucker, and Alfred "Duck" Mason, the Lucky Duck's owner and chief cook. He sat behind the soda fountain, his feet propped up, *Monday Night Football* flickering on a small television set he held on his aproned lap. Alfred would be no help.

"Now, let's get down to business, little lady," Rucker said abruptly. "You gonna threaten me anymore?"

With elegant ease, Dinah swiveled a cold look to him. *Little lady*, eh? "Doubtlessly not. I'd rather keep my council chamber possum free. I'd rather keep my peace of mind. I accept your apology. Just please don't pick on us anymore. I care about this town."

"I can see that," he said. "I like Mount Pleasant. I like

you. So let's talk about you." He looked comically smug. "I'm sure you know all about me."

"Oh, yes. I'd say you're exceedingly simple to understand."

He chuckled, the sound warm and rumbling. "I'm not simpleminded, if that's what you mean. And I'm really sorry for disruptin' everything tonight. And I'm really glad to meet you." He held out a hand. "Pals?"

Dinah squinted at his hand, trying to figure out his motives. Was he looking for the story that had never been revealed six years ago? By the way, Mayor, why did you run out on the Miss America shindig? Why does somebody like you give up glamour and fame for life in Quietville, USA? She took his hand slowly, exhaling as the calloused, hard grip closed around her fingers and sank gently into her palm.

"Don't let go," he whispered. Dinah's gaze shot to his face. He leaned forward, his grip tightening, his expression serious. "Don't pull away. It's hot, but it won't burn."

She swallowed with great difficulty and glanced over to make certain Alfred wasn't watching this bizarre scene. "I know something was going on between us in the meeting," she told Rucker frankly. "It gets lonely here, but I want you to understand that I'm not easily—"

"Tell me about yourself," he ordered in a low, cajoling voice. "I'm just gonna sit here and hold your hand, and you tell me whatever you think I ought to know."

"Why?" she demanded.

"Because I want to see what kind of woman lurks behind those smart blue eyes. A woman with a man friend somewhere in town?"

"No." His fingertips were drawing blunt lines of fire inside her palm. She tested his determination by gently trying to pull back. His forefinger pressed sensuously into the soft center of her hand, urging her to be still, to relax. Dinah swallowed hard and shifted uncomfortably on the old vinyl seat, her whole body warm. All right, I'll just . . . just humor him, she decided.

"Someone special anywhere?" he asked.

"No. You?"

"No man friends," he said drolly. "I ain't that kind of boy."

"You know what I—"

"Ex-wife. Found her in New York, left her in New York. Divorced four years ago. Back then I wrote the obits. I got work in Birmingham, took up writin' a column, and I got famous for reasons I can't begin to understand. Along with the fame I got a lot more than a normal share of female attention."

"Still getting it?" she asked, then realized how the question sounded. Pure amusement lit his eyes as she shook her head wearily. "Mr. McClure, I retract that—"

"I don't like singles bars, I'm not a cradle robber, and I turn up my nose at aggressive, independent women, so that leaves me sittin' at home alone a lot. Call me Rucker."

"Call you a saint, if one is to believe that sweet little story about your love life. By the way, 'aggressive' and 'independent' describe me . . . Rucker."

"Nah, you've got potential," he informed her. "Now look, I'm not gonna play games here. You and me, we were communicatin' like live wires for a while there tonight. I'm lookin' into your eyes and thinkin' about old-fashioned romance—"

"And a docile, dependent woman. How would you describe your ideal victim?"

He grinned slyly. His fingers curled and uncurled inside her hand, their intent even more intimate. "Oh, she always has dinner ready for me, she loves all the sports I love, she just lives to give me massages, she fetches and totes whenever my friends come over to play poker, she likes to mow the lawn . . ."

Dinah laughed helplessly, enjoying his blarney. "When I tell you about myself, you'll see that I don't fit that mold at all." Her traitorous fingers wanted to caress the top of his broad, lightly haired hand. She forced them to remain obedient.

"You've got potential," he insisted again, his eyes deadly serious under their teasing veneer. Dinah rested her chin in her free hand and studied him. "So talk," he ordered. "You teach high school, right?"

It was hopeless to evade his interrogation, and as long as it remained harmless she'd enjoy it. Dinah told him about getting her master's degree in political science at Mitchataw College, a small but respected school in central Alabama. She explained how she came to Mount Pleasant to take a job teaching history, fell in love with the town, and got involved in local politics.

"And the town fell in love with you, it looks like," he said when she finished. "I watched how people acted toward you in the meeting." His fingers reached out to brush their heat across the sensitive skin of her wrist.

"I suppose. I was elected mayor over the incumbent, Mervin Flortney. He wasn't much of a mayor. Now let go of my hand." Breathing a little fast, she tugged it away. He took it back.

"Good girl. How'd you do it?"

She sighed in exasperation. "I'm not a girl. I'm twenty-seven years old."

"I'm thirty-six, but I'm still a boy," he teased. "Don't get caught up in quibblin' over semantics."

"Big word, semantics. Congratulations."

He laughed heartily and gave her hand a joyful squeeze. "Talk, Madam Mayor. Did you bowl these folks over with big-city shenanigans? You were raised in Atlanta, weren't you?"

"Yes, I was raised in Atlanta. No, I didn't bowl anyone over with . . . shenanigans. Are you assuming that I just thrust my chest forward and made insipid speeches? We beauty queens have a few more resources than that, thank you. I work hard to understand this town's problems and I work hard to make them better."

"Calm down there," he said. "It's just curious to somebody like me, who grew up in . . . uhmmm . . . modest circumstances, as my public relations man puts it, that anybody would give up money and glory to teach high-school history in a real-life Mayberry." He looked over her head as if watching someone come in the diner's door. "Aunt Bee!" he called. "Opie! Come set a spell!"

Dinah fought to keep from smiling but lost. His fingers wound between hers, and she marveled at her unwillingness to rebuke him. If she were an impulsive woman, she'd ask Rucker McClure to stop tempting and start satisfying. But she wasn't. At the age of sixteen she'd won Miss Teen Atlanta on the basis of an oration titled "Pride, Prudence, and Perseverance—Our Faithful Friends." Though the speech seemed pitifully naive to her today, she could still recite it by heart.

"You don't understand why I love Mount Pleasant," she told him. "Let me tell you what life is like here."

He nodded. "Talk to me, Madam Mayor. I'm a good listener." Dinah felt an odd sense of camaraderie as she studied the sudden gentleness in his eyes. She hadn't talked to a man like this in a long, long time. Wait a minute. She'd never talked to a man like Rucker McClure before. A lovable maniac. Lovable?

"Well," she began, "let me tell you about our grand and exalted Possum Days Festival . . ."

With his throaty laughter as a backdrop, Dinah told him abut the festival, about Mount Pleasant High and the Mount Pleasant High Wildcats, state AA football champions in 1959 but never since then, about the Warp 'n' Weave clothing factory that employed three hundred residents, about the fall tourist trade that would begin in a week or so when the leaves started to turn. She told him the history of Mount Pleasant's World War I cannon, sitting bronzed and proud on the town square. She told him the history of the rose bushes planted around the cannon by the Mount Pleasant Women for a Progressive Future.

And somewhere along the way Rucker stopped being a stranger and became a friend. At about eleven o'clock Alfred set a pot of coffee and a plate of chocolate donuts on the table, then went back to his TV to watch the late news and Johnny Carson. A few truckers ambled in, but other than that the place was quiet. At midnight Rucker was deeply involved in telling Dinah a story about his father, a trucker who'd died in a dramatic highway accident when Rucker was fifteen. Dinah was deeply involved in watching Rucker, her coffee untasted, her donut half-eaten. At one A.M. Alfred shooed them and the truckers out, then locked up for the night.

Rucker kept talking as they walked down Main Street's oak-shaded sidewalk to where his car was parked. He also kept holding Dinah's hand. He swung it merrily, as if teasing her to believe that hand-holding was innocent.

". . . and so, when I made it big," he said, "I told Mama, 'You've been a waitress all your life, sweetheart, and you've worked damn hard. Now I'm gonna buy you the fanciest condo in Florida and you're gonna set down there by Mattie and her family—Mattie's my married sister—and you're gonna have more fun than a chicken at a worm farm.'"

"And what did your mother say?"

"Prrrr-ruck, cluck cluck cluck, prrrr-ruck."

They were still laughing as he held the Cadillac door for her. Dinah slid inside and looked around curiously at the plush interior. "A black Cadillac Seville," she murmured as he settled into the driver's seat. "I expected a custom pickup truck."

"Don't worry, I'm still a hayseed at heart." He handed her a sleek tape case from under the seat. "Pick something. I love music of all kinds."

"Ah, the soundtrack from *Deliverance*, 'Honky Tonk Favorites from Nashville,' 'Highlights from *Hee Haw*.' This is music of all kinds?"

"I have wide-ranging musical tastes," he said solemnly.

"Indeed. I'd say these tapes cover the range from country-western to country-western. With a little country-western thrown in. How will I ever choose? Ah. 'Banjo Favorites.' That sounds safe."

She started to put the tape in. Rucker leaned close to her as she did. "Who wants 'safe'?" he asked. Dinah twisted to face him, her breath catching as she inhaled his clean, masculine scent. No seductive, fancy colognes for this man. He didn't need help seducing women.

"I want 'safe,' " she whispered.

"Nah, you don't. I'm gonna kiss you." The tone was light, but his voice was husky. "But I'll keep it safe. For right now, anyway."

"You want me to kiss you right here on the street?"

"Nah. I'd rather you kiss me right here on the lips. Just aim for a spot about a smidgen below my mustache."

A flabbergasted laugh started in her throat and never surfaced. His kiss trapped it between them and turned it into a plaintive groan of pleasure and exasperation, mostly pleasure. Rucker slid both arms around her and brought her closer. Dinah raised shocked hands to grip his shoulders. She gripped, then relaxed, then gripped again harder, as his mouth made slow, erotic movements on hers. Suddenly her world was only taste and touch and smell, all of the sensations magnified by a haze of physical desire and shock.

The Fourth of July. A first kiss. Puppy love. All these notions got tangled up in her thoughts as her tongue touched his and sensation exploded across the skin of her abdomen and thighs. His hands rubbed her shoulder blades in circular patterns then slid down her spine, his fingers tracing the indention of bone and muscle even through her clothes.

Lost to his skilled seduction, Dinah wrapped both arms around his neck and leaned into the kiss, her back arching. His soft moan was vulnerable and gentle. Is there really a sensitive, sweet man under all the flirtatious macho humor? she wondered. Would it be wrong to be impulsive? Wasn't she entitled to ignore common sense with such an amazing man?

Dinah felt him tugging on her left jacket-sleeve. She inhaled raggedly as it started sliding down. The man is seducing me, she thought without much alarm. Right here on Main Street. He's seducing me, and I'm not lifting a finger to stop him. His hands kept up their wonderful assault on her lower back, slipping lower, lower . . . Wait a minute, her logical mind protested. Unless he had a third arm, a very unusual talent for magic, or a friend in the back seat, he couldn't possibly rub her rump with both hands and pull her jacket off one shoulder at the same time.

Dinah jerked her mouth away from his. "It's happenin' fast, I know," Rucker said soothingly, his lips brushing her cheek. "It's not wrong, though. Nothing's ever been so right—"

"I'm being attacked by something!"

"Me, too, hon. Isn't it wonderful?"

"No, no! Really attacked!" She twisted frantically and came face to face with the possum, which was clinging fervently to her shoulder. Dinah yelped and the possum squeaked. Then its eyes glazed over and it tumbled limply down her back onto the seat.

"You scared it!" Rucker said reproachfully. He reached around her and scooped the small animal into his hand. Dinah cringed away from it and slid into the far corner of the car, her pulse pounding desperately. Insanity had started with a torrid kiss and ended with a fainting marsupial. She gathered her senses for a moment, wondering what in the world had happened to her. Prudence had deserted pride and perseverance.

"It's playing possum, I assume?" she said coldly. She straightened her jacket with an authoritative tug.

"As a matter of fact, yes. Poor critter."

He stroked the limp little animal with obvious concern. Dinah's heart softened and she reached over to pet the possum too. After a moment it came to and wobbled upright.

"Mr. McClure, I'd like to go back to my car at city hall now, thank you. Your possum and I are in the same discombobulated state."

He reached out and stroked her cheek as languidly as he'd been stroking the possum's back. "Feel better?" he asked several seconds later. Her skin was fiery under his touch.

"I'm fine," she said. "Let's go."

"When can you and I—"

"Never. Please go back to Birmingham and don't make fun of me or my town anymore."

"Look here, Dinah, after that kiss—"

"That's all she wrote, Rucker. You're looking for a Playmate Slave of the Year, and I'm not interested."

"You're not givin' me a chance."

"Please. I don't want to discuss this anymore. I'm

sorry I got carried away and kissed you," she said firmly.

"Uh-uh. I don't believe that any more than I believe in TV weathermen. We'll just drive on back, and you calm down, and then we'll talk."

"We've finished talking. We've finished, period."

His face grim, he set the possum down between them and started the car. Music that sounded to Dinah like eight hundred dueling banjos—some of them dying from the duel, if their pitiful twangs were any indication—filled the car as Rucker drove back down Main Street.

"You just ran our red light," Dinah said.

"What red light?"

"Our only red light. And the police chief saw you. You'd better pull over."

An incredulous look on his face, Rucker glanced back at the traitorous red light that swung over the intersection by the Twittle County Courthouse. Lights flashing, a police car came after the Cadillac.

"I'm damned doomed," he said.

Police Chief Dewey Dunne was one of Mount Pleasant's most prominent black citizens, a Baptist deacon, and a stickler for rules. He tipped his hat to Dinah.

"Mornin', Dinah."

"Morning, Dewey."

"Morning, sir," Rucker echoed. Dewey scanned Rucker's driver's license with a scowl on his beefy face.

"This is expired, Mr. McClure."

"Nah. Let me . . . hmmmm . . . reckon so, sir."

"Where's your proof of insurance, Mr. McClure?"

Rucker winced. He turned to Dinah with beseeching eyes. "Haven't you got any clout?" he asked.

"Not with the chief," she answered primly. "Haven't you got an insurance card?"

"My washing machine washed it. It's currently stuck in the filter, in about two million soggy, little bitty pieces."

"Mr. McClure," Dewey intoned in the voice of God, "I'm afraid I've got to take you in."

"Nah, you don't. I'm with the mayor."

"That don't mean diddly to me, Mr. McClure," Dewey said politely. "Sorry, Dinah. Nothin' personal about that."

"I understand, Dewey," she answered. "But this once, couldn't you—"

"Out of the car, please, Mr. McClure."

Dinah closed her eyes in despair. Rucker McClure would wreak a terrible revenge in return for this escapade, she was certain. He'd hunt down every condemning, amusing thing he could find about Mount Pleasant and about her too. Mount Pleasant's reputation could survive such a war. Hers couldn't.

Dinah opened her eyes to find Rucker studying the distraught expression on her face. Exasperation and disbelief shown in his eyes, but humor quirked around his mouth. He handed her the possum. "Take care of our baby," he drawled. His voice was full of determination. "And tell him . . . tell him Daddy intends to learn all about this mean little town and its mayor. Just as soon as he gets off the chain gang."

Dinah clutched the baby possum to her stomach and nodded wearily. Her fate was sealed.

Two

"Hey, coach, how was that routine?" the captain of the Mount Pleasant Wildcat drill team called.

Seated on the hood of her small station wagon Dinah shielded her eyes from the late afternoon sun and nodded distractedly to the thirty girls lined up in the school parking lot. "You look great. Tomorrow we'll go down to the field and practice with the band. Run through it one more time."

Dinah rewound the tape in the boom box that sat beside her. The drill team snapped to attention, did a dress right, and began their routine to a marching-band version of *Thriller* that pounded out of the tape player. Anxious to get away from the jarring music, Dinah walked across the parking lot and stood at the edge of the stadium embankment, staring blankly down the long, steep hill at the football team practicing for Friday night's game.

As she'd done all day, she thought about Rucker McClure. He'd finally driven out of Mount Pleasant at two-thirty in the morning, possum in tow. His parting words to her had destroyed her sleep for the rest of the night: "Keep your heart open and your lips puckered. I'll be back." She'd answered dryly, "Bring proof of insurance."

The ear blasting version of *Thriller* ended, and Dinah walked wearily back to the car. "Let's call it a day," she told the drill team. "Good job." They began gather-

ing their purses and tote bags. Dinah put the tape
player in the station wagon's back seat then stacked its
cassettes in a shoe box with her usual precise attention to neatness. From the corner of her eye she glimpsed
a car pulling into the lot. A mom, no doubt. Then she
looked up.

She inhaled sharply. Not a mom. A McClure. Rucker
parked the sleek black Cadillac next to her dumpy
wagon and climbed out gracefully. Dinah caught her
breath and took a step backwards. In the bright light
of day the man affected her even more than he had last
night. He was tall, well built, confident, and totally
devastating, which was saying a lot, she thought, considering the state of his clothes. He wore another pair
of old jeans—or the same pair, who could tell—with an
Auburn University football jersey and the same gray
houndstooth sport jacket from before. Today he'd traded
his fancy black boots for jogging shoes. That fashion
decision must have taken him hours, she thought dryly.

Rucker ambled toward her, his best nonchalant expression in place, a jaunty smile fixed on his face, his
heart racing. She doesn't look mad to see me again. At
least that's a relief, he noted. She did look defensive,
though, sort of like a lady squirrel anxious to run for
the nearest tree. A beautiful lady squirrel, he added in
silent admiration.

Man, she had style. No other woman could look so
neat and yet so sexy in tan trousers, a yellow blouse,
and an argyle sweater vest. Her dark hair curled below
her shoulders in long, loose waves. He felt her cold blue
eyes trying to whittle his control away and knew they
were succeeding. Why does this woman mess up my
mind so bad? Rucker asked himself in annoyance. I'm
suave. I'm hot. I'm a celebrity. I'm—

"Well, Kemo Sabe, where's your possum?" Dinah asked
bluntly. He stopped right in front of her, closer than
she wanted him to be, too close for her to breathe
normally. He looked exasperated.

"Back at the motel."

"Which motel?"

"The Schwartz Mountain Motel," he told her. " 'Scuse

me, I mean the Schwartz Mountain Motel and Taxidermy Shop. Little lady, I hope my possum's gonna be safe alone."

She sighed. That chauvinistic *little lady* business again. "The Schwartz's will treat him and you better than you deserve."

He smiled crookedly. "Guests check in, but they never check out."

Dinah gave him a somber look. "You came back sooner than I expected."

"There are a million stories in the naked city. I'm settin' up my word processor here for a few days."

"Mount Pleasant isn't naked or a city. Please go back to the city." Her worry and sadness deepened. "I know you're going to take literary revenge on me. That's all right, but don't hurt anyone else, please."

He frowned, his green eyes clouding with anger. "Do you think I'm that kind of man? You think I've come up here to look for some sort of petty trash I can print?"

"You're a reporter. I know all about reporters."

"You don't know squat about me, Dinah," he said tersely.

She frowned, too, bewildered and even more defensive. "Then what do you want?"

His mouth thinned into a line of challenge. "Well, for starters, a kiss hello."

He bent forward quickly and stole one from her parted lips. Dinah gasped and he kissed her again. It took nearly five seconds for her to gather her mental faculties enough to step back. Five seconds of new shock and rebellious tingles. Dinah whirled around and discovered, as she'd expected, that they had an audience of thirty open-mouthed teenage girls.

"You didn't see that," she said firmly. "None of you saw that."

She turned back around and faced Rucker, her jaw set. "That was indefensible."

He arched one brow in his jaunty way, the way that told her he had already gotten over being mad and was now enjoying himself. "You didn't even try to defend yourself," he joked.

"I mean, you pig, that you can't justify what you did. I have a good reputation in this town—"

"Everybody knows you got a good reputation. Now they want you to have a good man. Lula Belle Mitchum told me so when I stopped by city hall on my way in. She told me you're the best coach the drill team ever had and she told me which way to the school to find you." He looked around at the sprawling, tree-shaded brick building that was Twittle County's only high school. "Looks like the one I went to," he noted. "Old and friendly."

Dinah huffed loudly. "Rucker, I don't care if you get every man, woman, and possum in this town on your side, my mission in life is not centered around satisfying your chauvinistic fantasies." His eyes settled on her with calm scrutiny. Dinah pointed an accusing finger at him. "If you're one of those vain men who's looking for a beauty queen to put on his arm, then you could do a lot better than me. I'm six years older and ten pounds heavier than when I paraded around as Miss Georgia, so—"

"What hurt you so bad that you curdled up and turned cynical?"

His harsh words put a clamp on her diatribe. She gazed up at him feeling guilty, all too aware that she had been unnecessarily cruel to him. "Life," she snapped. Dinah added silently, *And death.* Her father's death, a puzzling tragedy surrounded by shame and scandal. What would this aw-shucks journalist do if he discovered that she had played a prominent role in that juicy scandal?

Right now he gazed down at her with concern. "Ssssh," he crooned suddenly. Rucker reached out and smoothed a strand of her hair away from the autumn breeze. "Whatever it was, don't let it make you skittish around me." He touched her cheek in a brief, light caress then let his hand drop to his side. His unexpected gentleness in the aftermath of her sarcasm had a horrible effect on her control, and she looked away, brushing at her eyes with quick, embarrassed motions.

"I'm sorry," she whispered hoarsely. "I'm really sorry for being such a creep. When I was competing in pageants I had a lot of bad experiences with people who wanted to take advantage of me. Especially reporters. I'm sorry," she repeated. "Please don't take this out on my town."

He exhaled in dismay. "I'm not Rucker the Hun. I like small towns. I like the human interest stories I find in small towns. I want to write about this place. About Dewey and Lula Belle . . . and you. About the good things you do."

Dinah felt queasiness fighting for control of her stomach, and she took a moment to subdue it. She had to convince Rucker not to write about her. If his national column drew attention, if other reporters took an interest in an ex-beauty queen turned mayor, it would be disastrous.

"I'm not special," she murmured to Rucker. "I'm just trying to do what I think is right. I don't always succeed."

"You're very special. People look up to you. Lula Belle said so. You've earned a lot of affection and respect here."

She studied him in speechless consideration, her breath short. "It's nice that you think so," she told him.

"Will you put up with me for a few days? I just want to put your town on the map and make you a celebrity. Is that so bad?" He grinned.

Dinah swallowed hard. He sincerely wanted her company, and she sincerely needed his. She had to learn more about him if she was going to sidetrack his determination to publicize her life. She had to learn more about him, period.

She cleared her throat. "All right. How would you like to come to the VFW's monthly get-together? It's tonight, and I have to make a speech. The people are terrific, but the food's really horrible—canned spaghetti and hard garlic bread."

"When I was in college I lived on canned spaghetti," he said happily. "I love canned food. No fuss, no mess, no dishes. My china pattern is called 'Corrugated.' "

Despite her fears she chuckled. "The veterans will insist that you use a plate."

"I'll manage. Sounds like fun."

"Well, they'll be thrilled to have you there." She paused, gazing up at him with intrigue that she tried desperately to hide. It was wrong to feel so excited about this turn of events. It was wrong to feel so excited about this dangerous visitor. "You went to college?"

He grinned. "Auburn University, the South's finest. Took me seven years to get a degree in journalism, but then, when you're as good-lookin' as I am, you don't need brains."

"No, just humility. Seven years to get a bachelor's degree?" She'd gotten hers in three, and her master's degree in one.

"Well, for two and a-half years of that, I was in the Army."

"You were drafted?"

"Nope. I joined."

"No brains at all, I'd say."

"I believe in duty."

She started to laugh then saw that he was serious. Surprise and pride swelled inside her chest. "You have strong beliefs," Dinah said. "I admire that."

He couldn't bear to let the conversation turn solemn for long. Rucker gave her a rakish salute. "I believe in motherhood, patriotism, and fried chicken, but not necessarily in that order." He paused. "I also believe in puttin' women on a pedestal."

"Hmmmm. So you can look up their skirts."

Startled, he stared at her for a moment. Then a smile of absolute thrill lit his handsome face. "What a sense of humor," he sighed in sincere appreciation. "I've never met a woman who could retaliate so well."

Dinah quelled an urge to blush like an excited game-show matron who'd just been kissed by Bob Barker. This was the strangest compliment any man had ever given her, and yet she felt inordinately pleased by it. Everything was getting confused. He was nothing but trouble, and she was afraid of him. But she realized suddenly that she was glad he'd come back to Mount Pleasant.

"She's blushing, she's blushing," he chanted in a ridiculous adolescent tone. "I love it."

Dinah began to laugh hopelessly. Rucker wrapped a hand around her arm and tilted his head towards hers, laughing along with her. "You're easy to please," she said finally.

"You're easy to be pleased around," he whispered.

After a mild battle over who would pick up whom for the VFW spaghetti dinner, Dinah won. She wasn't going to let this persuasive, dangerous man come near her home, a small clapboard farmhouse hidden in a stand of pine trees a few miles from town. She had a feeling that if he ever got over the threshold, he'd never leave. She might never let him leave. And that would be foolish.

She was rarely late for anything—old beauty queen training, she thought wryly—so at precisely seven o'clock, the autumn darkness drawing slowly around her, Dinah parked her station wagon outside room number 4 of the Schwartz Mountain Motel and Taxidermy Shop, waved at David Schwartz, who was burning one last pile of leaves on the lawn that fronted the main office, and blew the horn for Rucker. After thirty seconds she blew again. The door banged open and he filled the frame, silhouetted by the cozy light of his bedside lamp.

Dinah acknowledged a decidedly feminine response to the outline of his body. His long legs tied in nicely to trim, muscular hips and a sturdy torso that widened into magnificent shoulders. His was the kind of body that just naturally drew women's eyes, no matter how haphazardly he clothed it. Rucker is living proof that grits ought to be the breakfast of champions, she thought. Her eyes widened as she saw the possum in his hands. He held it up proudly, as if it were his baby, then lifted one of its long, pink paws so that the slack-faced little animal appeared to be waving at her. Dinah nearly choked on laughter as she waved back.

He set the possum on the bed, shut the room's door, and walked gingerly toward her car, his boots in one hand. He settled into the passenger seat, and Dinah felt her pulse accelerate at the effect of his overwhelming presence in the small space.

"How do I look?" he asked cheerfully. "I was watchin' *Wheel of Fortune* when you drove up, and I hadn't put my boots on yet. Sorry." He waved large, angular hands at his outfit. "I don't know how to coordinate clothes. But this outfit usually does pretty well when I go someplace nice."

"What's *Wheel of Fortune?*"

He stared at her for a moment. "Great balls of fire, just the country's favorite game show. Dinah, what do you do up here at night in the mountains?"

"Read a good book or play the piano if I'm not busy doing something related to being mayor, which takes up a lot of my spare time."

"We're gonna have relationship problems if you don't like important stuff like *Wheel of Fortune,*" he told her drolly.

"We can't have relationship problems if we don't have a relationship. You enjoy doing this outrageous Redneck Everyman routine, don't you?"

He looked grandly perturbed. "Routine? Are you suggestin' that this is not my true personality?"

"I've done a lot of reading about you lately, dear boy. Gloria Steinem said you're—let's see, how did she put it—you're 'an irresistible red-clay phenomenon who loves to play devil's advocate.' She also said that she thinks you're Phil Donahue at heart."

"That woman's crazy," he groaned. "I'm Johnny Cash, or Willie Nelson, or Duke Wayne, God rest his fine soul—"

"Okay, okay, thou doth protest too much, me thinks," she soothed, chuckling.

She scanned his appearance from the feet up, her lips compressed in controlled amazement. "Be honest, Miss Dinah," he warned. "You got this polite, tactful little expression on your face, sort of like you're still Miss Georgia and some rude yokel just asked you what color undies you wear. Tell the truth. What do you think? Am I handsome, or what?"

"You're an egomaniac, that's what." She sighed. "Well, you have on one brown sock and one black sock."

"Whoops. No one can see 'em under my boots."

"And frankly, brown corduroy trousers do not make a fashion statement when combined with a gray houndstooth jacket, a white shirt, and—good grief, has that tie been washed in mud?"

"The catalog called it nut brown," he protested, chuckling. "It was on sale."

"Spend a whole dollar next time."

"Ouch. You mean, vicious,"—he grasped both her hands and pulled her toward him, his voice dropping to a throaty level—"gorgeous, sexy, funny . . ."

"No, no, no . . ."

"Yes, yes, yes . . ." He kissed her hard, deliciously hard, his tongue teasing at her lips until she gave in and allowed it to slip deep inside her mouth. It tickled and cajoled, then coaxed her tongue to play too. Dinah's hands clutched at his with trembling fierceness. His fingers wound through hers and he pulled her arms around his waist. His warm, masculine scent was tantalizing.

"Hold on tight," he whispered breathlessly. "We're gonna do something strange, but you're gonna love it. You need it. You need it bad."

"Not here . . . Rucker . . ." Alarmed, she started to pull away. Then she felt his hand on the back of her head, guiding it down to his big shoulder.

"We're gonna snuggle for a minute," he explained. He stroked her hair and slid one arm around her back. "Mmmm. Isn't this nice? This is the best way to get to know each other."

"Snuggle? Hug?" His shoulder felt wonderful, a perfect cushion for her cheek. "I was afraid you intended—"

"Yeah, I know you were afraid. Ssssh. I'm nobody to be afraid of. I'm a good old boy, you know, and that's almost the same as bein' an old-fashioned gentleman." He stroked her hair with long, languid motions, his fingers pressing intimately against her scalp.

"That's not what I meant. I'm not afraid of you or any other man. I'm not a simpering girl."

"Cautious, then," he corrected. "I know a woman like you is used to havin' her pick of men, but I also figure you've been hit on by a lot of turkeys." He paused. "I'm not a turkey, even if I am hittin' on you." His fingers curved around the nape of her neck, massaging. He turned his head just enough to let his warm breath brush her cheek and heat her skin.

"No, I don't think you're a turkey." Dinah blinked slowly, amazed at the easy way he made her bones melt. She wanted to snuggle closer. She wanted to tilt her head up and press a sample kiss against the skin of his throat. "I know all about turkeys," she whispered. "I had an ace turkey back when I was in college. After I walked out on the Miss America competition we broke up."

"So, bein' a brilliant journalistic type, I deduct that this bird was one of those vain men you mentioned earlier. He liked havin' a beauty queen for an ornament, huh?"

"That was part of it. And he never forgave me for giving up a shot at Miss America. He never understood."

"I don't understand it either."

Dinah inhaled sharply, and all her reserve rushed back. She tensed and sat back rigidly. "I'll explain it sometime. Not right now. Right now I have to regain my good sense and get us both to the VFW hall. You're a treacherous and seductive passenger."

"Aw, phooey." He loosened his grip reluctantly and let her return to her side of the car. "One last kiss."

"Mr. McClure—"

"Ooooh, I like it when you talk prissy and formal to me." He caught her chin in one hand, leaned forward, and planted a big, firm kiss on her mouth.

"Recalcitrant maniac!" she blustered, nearly smiling.

He kissed her again, twisting his mouth into hers. "Hmmm. Recalcitrant. Maniac. More. More."

Laughing and giddy, she pushed him away. "S-stop! Ludicrous—"

"Uh-huh, uh-huh?" He inched toward her, waiting wickedly for more provocative language.

"You tease . . . Rucker . . . good grief . . ." Dinah simply sputtered to a stop. He looked disappointed. She was gasping for breath.

"Phooey," he said again. He slumped back in his seat but stretched one arm along the top. His big, supple hand rested against her right shoulder, his fingertips very close to the bare skin of her neck. "You behave, bub," he told his hand drolly, "unless she starts coaxin' us with big words again."

Slightly addled and feeling as if she were a gas stove and he had turned all her burners on high, Dinah faced forward and started the car. She wondered briefly what good it did to have a high IQ if she couldn't even figure out how to keep from adoring a lunatic who was all wrong for her.

The local VFW contingent held its get-togethers at the huge, green community hall in the basement of Mount Pleasant's Methodist Church. Since there were only about a dozen veterans, they and their wives tended to look pitifully lost in the giant, antiseptic room. A pair of long tables were set up at the room's far end, Styrofoam cups neatly marking each person's dinner spot. As she and Rucker entered, Dinah forced a smile as bright as the painfully bright overhead lights. Their footsteps tapped loudly on the old white floor covering.

"The first time they invited me to dinner I went home afterwards and cried for an hour," she whispered to Rucker. "They seem so forgotten in this place."

An absolutely ancient little woman in a print dress tottered out of the church kitchen carrying a pan of garlic bread, which she set on a small folding table neatly draped with a cheap-looking paper tablecloth. The veterans stood around holding their decorated VFW caps. Dinah felt Rucker's hand comfortingly stroke the back of her blue cowl-necked dress. It made intriguing sensations radiate down her spine.

"Don't feel sorry for them," he said. "They're alive and kickin' and they got lots of pride. They're doin' just fine."

That insightful observation and the compassionate tone in his deep voice touched her deeply, and she turned her head to look at him as they approached the VFW group. "You're secretly philanthropic," she told him.

"I was raised Methodist."

Dinah swallowed a chortle and glanced at him. The slight crinkling of the laugh lines around his eyes was the only indication that he was restraining his own laughter.

"Well, lookee who we got here!" a frail, lanky man in a blue suit exclaimed. He came toward them, a dark wooden cane supporting his right side, and tipped his head to Dinah. "Glad to have you, Mayor." That formality over, he ignored her to turn a delighted gaze at Rucker. "And I know who you are!"

"A party crasher," Rucker answered jovially. "I came to eat your spaghetti and chase your women."

"Whoo whee! I saw you on Johnny Carson. You looked fatter."

"I had a swelled head."

Laughing inwardly, Dinah finally managed an introduction. "Mr. Jones, I'd like you to meet the infamous Rucker McClure, chief curmudgeon and bottle washer at *The Birmingham Herald/Examiner.* Rucker, this is Notley Jones, Mount Pleasant's retired postmaster and commander of this VFW post."

Rucker shook Notley's blue-veined hand. Other people gathered around, tittering excitedly. "Mr. McClure, we'd sure be thrilled if you'd make the after-dinner speech," Notley declared. "I know the Mayor won't mind. She gets to talk all the time anyhow."

"Just like a woman, isn't it?" Rucker said coyly. Dinah rolled her eyes in good-natured disgust. Rucker nodded. "I'll be glad to say a few words."

Dinah couldn't resist. "He only knows a few words, and most of them are very simple."

"Then we'll like him real fine," Notley answered, having missed the joke. Dinah could tell that Rucker enjoyed her failed barb immensely.

As they got in line to the buffet table he gazed down at her with gleaming eyes. "I'm in my element here, lady," he warned. "You're just jealous 'cause I'm beloved."

"Hah. I'm not jealous. And you're bewitched, not beloved. I know that you make big bucks as a speaker."

"Aw, I'm just the George Jessel of the peanut circuit."

"Don't be humble and play it down. I read that you get two thousand dollars a pop for what you're giving away tonight, so if you want me to make some excuse to get you out of speaking . . ."

"I can't be mean to these old sweeties. I'd rather be beaten with a stick or forced to listen to that silly Camphor flute player than hurt their feelings."

Her heart melted with more unfettered affection. "Camphor flute player?" she demanded. "What in the world are you talking about?"

"That guy who advertises his records on Ted Turner's TV station. He plays one of those funny little flutes, like somebody out of a Greek fairy story. His name's Camphor."

"Greek fairy story? Do you mean Greek mythology?"

"Same difference."

"Camphor, Camphor . . ." she thought for a moment. "Zamfir?" she asked incredulously. "You mean Zamfir, the internationally known musician?"

"Yeah, I guess that's him. Zamfir, Camphor, whatever. I think he's a con artist passin' himself off as a musician. Him and his goofy little handful of pipes."

Dinah called all her self-discipline into play to prevent the Mount Pleasant VFW from seeing their elegant mayor guffaw and slap her knees like a farmhand. Tears of hilarity crowded her eyes and she pressed shaking fingers to her smile to hold the sputtering sounds that threatened to erupt from her throat. She'd always pictured her ideal man as a perfect blend of the intellectual and artistic, a Renaissance man with exquisite taste and style. So why was she having the time of her life with Rucker McClure?

He spoke for twenty minutes after dinner, his hands shoved casually into his trouser pockets, that mellow southern voice of his flowing easily through the big room. Dinah propped her chin on one hand and looked up at him in awe, marveling at the quiet power he radiated and his natural ability to weave emotions into the simple stories he told. He talked about the responsibilities associated with freedom, the meaning of individualism, and the importance of taking pride in oneself and one's work.

He wasn't an intellectual and he didn't care about subtleties; his vision of the good life was so uncomplicated that it would have made the great philosophers hoot with condescending laughter. But she knew that Rucker's humorous, positive views were, in their own way, sophisticated and profound. They were exactly what the world needed, exactly what she needed. When he finished she saw tears in the eyes of the people listening to him and felt tears in her own eyes.

"You should have been a minister," she told him as they walked across the dimly lit church parking lot. The night was fragrant and the temperature pleasantly cool. A breeze rustled the giant oak trees that surrounded the lot, and Dinah inhaled the wonderful scent of wood smoke from distant hearth fires. "Or a politician," she added.

"I think I'd have made a good tractor salesman," Rucker answered. "I can talk the ears off a snake."

She smiled and inhaled again, feeling peaceful. It was odd that she was so comfortable around him now. She supposed that his speech had hypnotized her. Or that the man himself had. "Isn't it beautiful out here tonight?" she murmured. Dinah tilted her head back and looked up at a star-filled sky.

"Hmmm. Beautiful place, beautiful company." He took her hand.

"You're a seductive rascal, you know that?"

"I have your best interests at heart. You might never find a suitable man up here in the hinterland. You gotta import a man from somewhere else."

"You, I assume?"

He clicked his tongue and arched one brow wickedly. "I'm a good choice. I could rough up those smooth edges of yours. Make you a little more wild. That'd be good for you."

"It sounds painful."

A smile crooked one corner of his mouth, and he looked at her through half-closed eyes. "Not the method I had in mind. It'd be anything but painful."

"Come along, you determined flirt. Let's go sit on that bench over there and look at the stars. The view is wonderful."

The bench was just beyond the edge of the parking lot, under a maple tree. The Methodist church sat on a high ridge along with the rest of Mount Pleasant, and they could see a panorama of dark forest and scattered house lights. A slivered moon hung over the horizon. "God took some extra time with this night," Rucker commented softly.

Dinah gave him a pensive, charmed look. Then she sat down, faced forward, and studied the sky. He sat close beside her, still holding her hand. "Where do you live? In Birmingham?" she asked quietly. "I can't picture you in a city."

"You're not gonna believe this, but I've got a swank house in a country club subdivision. The suburbs. Got a swimmin' pool, got lawyers and doctors for neighbors, got a gardener, got a lady who comes in once a week to keep me neat."

"She must bring a blow torch," Dinah teased.

He chuckled. "I know you suspect I'm a pig, but I keep a very clean house. You should see my office at the newspaper, though. My secretary says it looks like a graveyard for old golf clubs. It's a mess."

"You play golf?" She turned to gaze at him quizzically.

He nodded. "Love it."

"You're a fascinating person, you know that? Just when I think I have you stereotyped, you confuse me. You ought to pitch horseshoes or bowl, not play golf. And you ought to live in a house trailer and drive a pickup truck. That's what I expected."

"Am I a disappointment?"

"Oh, not at all." She said that a little too fervently and looked away, biting her lower lip. His hand closed tighter around her own.

"You're not a stereotype either, Madam Mayor. I figured any woman who'd devoted so much time to bein' a beauty queen would have the brains of a frog."

"Hmmmph!" She echoed his earlier words. "Am I a disappointment?"

"No. I like smart women. I married one once."

Dinah spoke carefully. "And she was interviewed for a magazine piece on you. One of my students brought me a copy today. I read part of it at lunch."

Now he faced forward, and Dinah watched the moonlight follow the straight, tense lines that formed in his features. "What'd you think?" he asked after a long moment.

"She was awfully tough on you, although she did say you have talent. Funny, though. I couldn't see anything particularly condemning. The part about your three-day poker game in the locker room with the New York Knicks was sort of endearing." Dinah paused. "She said your views on marriage had all the sophistication of a country western song."

"Yeah." Rucker let go of her hand. He leaned forward, idly selected a twig from the ground between his feet, and rested his elbows on his knees. His head down, he slowly began snapping the twig into tiny pieces. When he spoke again, his voice was low and strained. "I thought we should try and make it work, but there was nothing left."

After a moment of amazement Dinah tilted her head and studied him tenderly. She tentatively reached out and rested her hand on his shoulder.

"Long time ago. Doesn't hurt anymore," he grunted.

"Caveman, if it means anything to you, I thought your basic lovableness showed through."

He twisted his head, and his eyes narrowed in a puzzled frown. "It did?"

Dinah couldn't help herself. She leaned forward and kissed his cheek. She knew that wasn't wise, but for the moment she didn't care. "It did," she whispered.

"Well, I'll be," he murmured. "You really think so."

The night was suddenly alive with emotion. Dinah hesitated for a sensible moment, then gently pressed her mouth to his. He shuddered with delighted surprise and took her in his arms. They leaned against the back of the bench, kissing each other slowly and thoroughly. He wrapped her hard against his chest, and when his mouth moved roughly down her neck she let her head droop back.

"You taste so sweet!" he gasped hoarsely, his lips on her throat. "What I could do for you, Dinah. What I *would* do for you . . ."

The hot, jumbled sensations inside her body made her clench the lapels of his coat for safety. "Snuggle," she implored. "Stop. Please . . . please. I'm not ready . . . for anything . . . like this."

"Stop," he agreed raggedly. He held her and she nestled her head into the crook of his neck. Rucker turned his head so that his cheek rested against hers, his mustache tickling her skin. "This is a helluva fantastic first date."

"This isn't a date," she argued. "It's . . . I don't know what it is."

"But you know what it's gonna lead to if I hang around your town a few more days," he murmured.

"I have a vague idea," she whispered weakly. "I make no guarantees."

"Want me to leave?"

"Would you leave if I asked you to?"

"Of course not."

Dinah laughed in resignation. "Then I might as well not ask."

"I sure am glad you're so smart."

"There's nothing smart about this. Two people who barely know each other, who are so different . . ."

"Who need each other," he countered. "Who fit together like two spoons in a tray. Who knew that the first night they laid eyes on each other."

"I laid eyes on a man with a possum on his head."

He sighed confidently. "I'm just perfect. I admit it."

She placed a hand over the center of his chest and let the reverberation of his soft laughter send pleasant ripples through her body. Dinah began to laugh too. Moonlit nights were meant for lunacy, she assured herself. Tomorrow she'd get back to normal.

Three

"And he said he'll never eat any food that's still wearing its overcoat," chortled Myra Faye Hayes, the algebra teacher. "That includes enchiladas and oysters."

A rousing chorus of laughter went up around the table in the teachers' lounge. Dinah sat down and opened her container of tuna salad. "I can only assume," she said dryly, "that you're discussing Rucker McClure." In the bright, crisp light of day, last night's temptation seemed very removed from reality. Had she really had such a splendid time?

Don Barkley, the shop teacher, nodded happily over his baloney sandwich. "He's my kind a' man. He wrote in that book of his, *Loving a Dixie Gal*, that the ideal woman is an excheerleader who majored in home ec at college. She has a beehive hairdo, and wears high heels at all times."

More laughter. Dinah's lips flattened into a thin line. She popped the tab on her diet soft drink and frowned, not having heard this particular information about Rucker's taste in women before. Yes, it was amazing what moonlight, fragrant autumn air, and expert masculine lips could do to her good sense.

"I like the characters he writes about in his column," noted Gita Smith, the English teacher.

"Oh? What characters?" Dinah asked nonchalantly.

"Well, there's Miss Hunstomper, his secretary. He

says she used to be a female wrestler. Then there's his five-hundred-pound Aunt Clara Vanette—Aunt Clarinet—who felt a lump in her couch and finally figured out that it was her long-lost parakeet. She recalled the night he disappeared, the night she took a nap on the couch with him perched on her shoulder. Poor, squashed thing—"

"Oh, please," Dinah begged, "not during lunch."

"I like his accountant, Ed Howe," interjected Byron Breedlove, head of the science department. "Of the firm Dewey, Cheatum, and Howe."

Everyone laughed again. "I like the Reverend Snooker Hornswaggle, his poker buddy," Myra Faye said.

Gita, a petite little brunette, giggled mightily. "Rucker said in one column that any woman over size eight ought to be sent to Russia. Isn't that funny?"

A booming, unmistakable voice filled the small lounge. "Looks like a mean group to me. Probably drink their beers warm and kick their dogs."

Dinah stood up, her mouth opening in amazement. "Speak of the devil."

Rucker grinned at her from the doorway, a bag from the local fast-food chicken franchise perched in the crook of one arm. "Good afternoon, teacher. I brought you some lunch."

He ambled in, looking quite handsome despite the fact that his auburn hair was tousled and he wore jeans, a Masters Tournament T-shirt, and an old green windbreaker. His eyes roamed greedily over her and her tasteful gray suit, then took in everyone else. Dinah put her hands on her hips and stared at him in amused exasperation. "Did anyone give you permission to come upstairs to the teachers' lounge?" she asked finally.

"Sure. My buddy Lou Parker."

"You never told me that you knew our principal."

He set the bag of food down and kissed her quickly on the cheek. Dinah put a fingertip on the warm, tingling spot and tried to ignore the slack-jawed looks the other teachers gave her. "I met him ten minutes ago," Rucker explained. "Now we're good friends. He said I could come on up here and make myself at home."

Dinah shook a finger at him. "What did you . . ."

Rucker smiled sweetly. "I promised to speak at the Friday afternoon pep rally."

"You are such a con man." He nodded, unashamed. She gave him a fiendish look. "Tell me something, dear boy. Did you once write that any woman larger than a size eight ought to be shipped to Russia?"

He didn't answer, and she could almost see the wheels turning in his mind. He formed a comical, shifty-eyed expression. "What size are you?" he asked.

"A perfect size ten, buster."

"I said any woman over a size sixteen ought to be shipped to Russia," he lied confidently.

"Hey!" Myra Faye, easily a size twenty and then some, waved a piece of celery at him with fake threat.

He grasped his heart. "Uh, I said," Rucker corrected, "that any woman over a size thirty . . ."

Everyone broke into chortles. "Sit down and remove your foot from your mouth," Dinah urged. She took a seat across the room and he followed her. He began pulling containers from the sack he'd brought. "Thank you," she murmured, staring at fried chicken, potato salad, pecan pie, and biscuits. "This is fattening. Fattening and unexpected." Everything about Rucker was unexpected, so she wasn't surprised.

"Well, I was down at Fred's barber shop, and I mentioned what my favorite food is, and Fred told me to go to the Captain Cluck place out on the highway, and when I got there, I thought, 'I bet Dinah likes fried chicken, and I know my possum does, too . . .'"

"What were you doing at Fred's?"

"Playin' poker." He smiled gleefully. "I won fifty matches. Fred won't be lightin' any candles for a while."

"And tell me, Mr. McClure, how else does a famous writer spend his work day?"

"Well, I got up real early and watched Oprah Winfrey. Then I went over to the Lucky Duck and had breakfast, and then I interviewed Bascom Lewis—"

"Bascom? To put it politely, Rucker, he's the town

wino. We sent him to a rehabilitation program, but it didn't do much good. What is so fascinating about Bascom?"

Rucker handed her a chicken breast and took a big bite from a biscuit. He chewed heartily, his green eyes completely content to do nothing but gleam at her with unabashed admiration. Then he swallowed and said, "He and me sat at the town square a while and shot spit balls at the cars on Main Street. He tells great stories. He's a very happy, contented man. He gets a pension from the Army and he—"

"You shot spit balls?" Her eyes widened in disbelief. "Do you enjoy provoking people everywhere you go?"

"Well, we didn't hit anything but a furniture truck from Mobile," Rucker protested. "And only because it was movin' slow."

Dinah shook her head in resignation. "And what sophisticated business do you have planned for the afternoon?"

"Well, I'm gonna drive down to Birmingham and play a little golf with the mayor there, then I'm comin' back here to go dove huntin' with Dewey tonight." He sighed. "I have to find something to do, since you're gonna ignore me and spend your evening at a city budget meeting."

"The chief? You made friends with my police chief and he's taking you dove hunting?"

"Sure. I want to ask him what it's like to be a black chief of police in Alabama."

"Do you even like to hunt?"

"Of course!" He looked grandly offended. "I'm a real man, right?"

"No doubt. I recognize it by the mustache."

He smiled crookedly. "Well, okay. I'll tell the truth. I haven't been huntin' since I was a kid. I'm not too good at it." He paused. "Actually, I couldn't even bag a bird at a restaurant." He lowered his voice. "Don't mention anything about my huntin' to the possum."

She chewed her chicken distractedly and basked in the glow of his vibrant personality and outrageous humor. "So what time do you want me to come for dinner tomorrow?" he asked abruptly.

Dinah coughed, dabbed at her mouth with a napkin, and eyed him askance. "You weren't invited."

"Never stopped me before." He looked plaintive. "Me and the possum can't eat a lot of restaurant food. We're delicate."

"Like a Mack truck is delicate." She fumbled with her fork, absently raking it across a cup of greasy potato salad that Rucker apparently thought was wonderful. All right, calm down, she told her skipping heart. Let him come to dinner. Show him that you're in charge of your wild fantasies and don't intend to be bowled over by his charm. His incredible charm. "How about seven o'clock? But I can't promise that you'll like my cooking. I don't cook southern." Dinah glanced wickedly at her fellow teachers, then looked back at Rucker. "How would you like some baked oysters, or maybe some enchiladas?"

"Great," he said enthusiastically. "I can't wait."

When they finished lunch he grasped her hand, squeezed it hard, winked at her, and stood up. "I'll see you tomorrow night," he promised. "Enchiladas or oysters. Hot damn."

Dinah stood also and squeezed his hand back. She realized with a sinking feeling that she was already anticipating their dinner together. She had to get herself under control before then.

"Be careful when you go hunting," she told him.

He looked so happy at her concern that she squeezed his hand one more time before she let it go. Rucker said a pleasant good-bye to the rest of her group and strode out the door whistling.

Gita stared after him, sighing blissfully. "He doesn't care if you're a size ten and he's willing to eat oysters and enchiladas for you. Oh, Dinah, this is so romantic."

"I think," Nureyev said loudly, "therefore I am!" He preened a little and chanted that bit of philosophy several more times. Finally Dinah turned away from the kitchen sink and tossed him a slice of mushroom to stop his chattering. He caught it deftly in his sharp black beak, shook it several times to make certain that it was dead, and swallowed it. Then he screeched happily.

"I'll cart you and your perch out to the back porch if you don't quiet down," she warned. "One talkative male in this house will be enough tonight."

She checked the casserole dish in the oven, turned the heat down under a pot of tiny potatoes on the stove, then hurried through the house, nervously fluffing pillows and checking for dust devils. When she realized how uncharacteristic her housekeeping frenzy was, she stopped abruptly and declared to the fieldstone fireplace, "I am not doing this for Rucker McClure's benefit! I have nothing against cheerleading, beehive hairdos, or home ec degrees, but they aren't my style!"

She heard the sound of the Cadillac crunching up her gravel driveway. Dinah trotted to the baby grand piano, which occupied one corner of the living room, and sat down. She gave her white slacks and brightly colored pullover a quick perusal, made sure her French braid extended neatly down the center of her back, then rested her fingers on the piano keys and began playing a Chopin piece. She knew exactly what picture she wanted to present when Rucker stopped on her porch and looked through the glass panes of the front door. Casual, elegant intimidation. Watch your step, Mr. McClure.

She kept her face composed and serene when she heard his heavy footsteps on the whitewashed plank porch, and she kept playing with outward patience until his cheerful rapping signaled that the show had begun.

Grace Kelly, eat your heart out, Dinah thought proudly as she slowly raised her head to look at him. He had a large grocery bag in one hand, and the possum was perched on his shoulder. She sighed. Who could deal intelligently with a man who thought of a possum as a fashion accessory?

Through the glass panes he gave her approach a sensual inspection so hot it could have dissolved steel. Tendrils of tickling sensation exploded in her stomach and spread downward. Stop seducing me, you Southern Don Juan, she begged silently. One corner of his mouth rising into a smile, he held up a hand, wrist relaxed, and shook it. Hubbah hubbah, chicky, the gesture told her. Nice tomatoes. It wasn't quite the humble, intimidated response she'd hoped to evoke.

But it was sincere, sexy, and effective—so effective that Dinah's body felt deliciously languid even as she rolled her eyes in exasperation. Decorum gone, she put a hand on her hip, swung the door open, and looked at him wryly.

"So you and Dewey didn't come back until after lunch today," she said with mild rebuke. "And both of you had hangovers. And no doves."

He nodded, looking a little sheepish. "I forgot how fast news travels in a small town. We had a good time, though. He's a great character. The best Baptist deacon I've ever known."

"Come in before I lose all my heat from the fireplace."

"I wouldn't want you to lose all your heat," he noted smoothly as he stepped inside. She closed the door and watched him look around the big, open living room at the piano, the mixture of abstract and classical art, the white-on-white contemporary decor, and the bookcases filled to overflowing. "This is some farmhouse," he observed.

"I did some renovating and redecorating. Make yourself at home. Give me your coat."

"I never had a home like this." He handed her the grocery bag and the possum, then shucked off the same windbreaker he'd worn the day before. Underneath it, his soul stirring body was covered in a fresh selection from his collection of plaid shirts and jeans.

"Beer?" she asked, forcing her traitorous eyes to the grocery bag.

"Champagne. Hah. Surprised you, didn't I?"

"I didn't know our package store carried champagne. Everyone got excited last year when the owner brought in some twenty-dollar bottles of wine. People went in just to look at them."

"Ah, but I went to Birmingham yesterday, you recall. The big city. I bought it there. The best champagne, of course. Or at least, it cost the most."

"Well . . . well, thank you. It's very nice." Feeling awkward and pleased, she set the possum down on her carpet and took Rucker's jacket. "I'll go put it in the refrigerator."

"The champagne, not my jacket," he requested coyly.

"Right," she mumbled.

"You're forgetting something, Miss Dinah."

She took a step backwards, clutching the grocery bag in front of her. "No, I didn't," she said lightly.

His eyes were too serious, his mouth too enticing. "Yes, you did." He cupped her face in both hands and watched her lips part in expectation as he stepped closer. "That's the kind of reaction I like to see," he whispered, and kissed her. "Hello." He kissed her again, his tongue sweeping inside her mouth. "You look fantastic." Another kiss. "I missed you." A final kiss, damp and intimate, and by now she was leaning forward, her breath ragged and her eyes closed tightly. He nibbled the corner of her mouth. "I didn't know you could play the piano, Madam Mayor. Takes sensitive fingers to do that. Wish I were a piano."

He nuzzled her neck from shoulder to ear, tickled her earlobe with his mustache, then ran his fingers over her cheek bones and down to her lips. He caressed their sensitive surface with his fingertips while she let her eyes open languidly. His voice was throaty, and his chest moved in a quick rhythm that matched her own. "Will you tickle my ivories after dinner, Deedee?"

Blinking groggily, Dinah stepped back. "Deedee?" she rasped. "Deedee?"

"Yeah. It's a good nickname. How do you like it?"

She stood silent for a moment, catching her breath, trying to think straight. Finally she managed to say, "I have not, nor shall I ever be, a 'Deedee.' That name conjures up images of a tiny person in ruffles and heavy mascara."

"Well, I can dream, can't I?" he joked.

Dinah put a hand to her forehead to test for cracks. No, she only *felt* as if she were falling apart and enjoying every second of it. "You, sir, may call me 'Dee,' if you insist."

"Okay. I can compromise."

"What may I call you, Rucker?"

"How about honey bunny, or handsome, or sweetcakes? 'Your Majesty' will do. That's what my secretary uses."

"She's obviously unqualified to find a job elsewhere, poor desperate woman."

She turned and hurried toward the kitchen, her knees still shaky from the effect of his kisses. Laughing, Rucker followed her. "Actually, she gives me no respect at all. She's studying for a degree in psychology at night school. She's a little bitty blond who served three years in the Navy. I used to protect her from the he-wolves at the paper, until I found out she has a black belt in karate and a wit like sharp steak knives."

"Is this the fabled Miss Hunstomper?"

"Yeah."

"Buon giorno!" Nureyev called from the kitchen. *"Nein! Sprechen sie Englisch, amigo?"*

"This is my pet crow," Dinah explained as she stepped across the threshold. "His name is Nureyev." She paused for smug effect. "After the ballet star. You'll have to pardon him. He gets his foreign languages confused."

Rucker paused, staring in amazement at the large black bird sitting on a perch stand by the room's bay window. "I have the same problem," he commented vaguely. He tracked Dinah's graceful movements around the airy, windowed kitchen, watching her put the champagne in the refrigerator and then go into the dining room beyond. She came back with a crystal snifter half full of dark liquid.

"How about some brandy and soda?" she asked.

He took it wordlessly, and the gleaming amusement in her blue eyes alerted him that she was enjoying his intrigue over the crow. "It came from Arnold Westerby," she finally explained. "He's a ranger down at the county forestry station. He found it as a baby and brought it to me. I never knew crows could talk, but they can. And they're very intelligent." She paused. "Arnold brought me the possum too. I think Arnold has a crush on me."

Rucker took a swallow of the smooth brandy and regained his aplomb. "Now, how can I compete with a feller who gives you crows and possums?" he asked wryly. "I've got animal tendencies, but not that kind."

Dinah glanced at him, but said nothing. She opened the oven door and removed a beautiful white casserole dish. "I hope you like coq au vin."

"Ohhhh, chicken and vegetables in wine sauce. I can deal with that."

Dinah looked at him in surprise. He arched one brow. "I've been in lots of nice restaurants. I know what coq au vin is. Hah."

"Mr. McClure, you outshine all my expectations." She fluttered her eyelashes. "Of course, I didn't expect much."

He bowed. At that point, the possum waddled into the kitchen. *"Nein! Nein!"* Nureyev screeched, eyeing the newcomer in dismay. "I think, therefore I am!"

"I sleep, therefore I am," Rucker responded. Sighing, he bent over and picked the possum up gently. "Come on, little feller, I'm gonna set you free out in Dee's woods."

Dinah turned from the stove and studied the sorrowful expression on Rucker's face. "Why?"

"Well, I don't know if he's happy bein' a pet. I want to give him up before I get any more attached to him."

"When I sent him to you, I assumed you'd have someone turn him loose the same day. I never expected you to keep him."

Rucker set his brandy down on the kitchen's round oak table and stroked the little animal's head. "He's ugly and dumb. That sort of appeals to me." Dinah felt a swell of sympathy. The man actually looked distraught over the idea of giving up the least lovable mammal God ever created. "Which way to the back door?" he asked sadly.

"Through the living room."

He left, and when he returned five minutes later, he

was possumless. "Little feller disappeared right into some honeysuckle bushes," Rucker noted. He sat down at the kitchen table and tried to look stoic.

Dinah couldn't resist such sincere, if bizarre, melancholy. She walked over to him, bent forward, and kissed him lightly on the mouth. "Everything's on the table, honey bunny," she murmured. "Come and drown your sorrows in boozed-up chicken."

They talked, the mood quiet and relaxed, during dinner. She told him about her mother, who had preceded her as a Miss Georgia. Julie Sheridan, then Julie Meredith, had held the title in 1950. She had died of meningitis when Dinah was fifteen. Afterwards, Dinah's father had devoted all his emotional energy to molding his daughter into the same image.

"My father wasn't manipulative," Dinah explained. "Mother had wanted to be Miss America, but never made it. Father thought the best way to honor her memory was to help me win what she'd always envied. I wasn't interested in beauty pageants at first, but then I got caught up in the competitive spirit."

"How many pageants did you win?" Rucker asked.

"Well, I started when I was fifteen and stopped when I was twenty-one, so about"—she paused, estimating—"forty. Out of about sixty."

"I'm impressed."

"The first was Miss Gum Spirits. I represented the Georgia turpentine industry."

He groaned. "You were a real trooper. You must have all sorts of funny trophies."

"They're all packed away." She shrugged. "I won't kid you. It stopped being enjoyable after I won the Miss Georgia title. I used to smear mentholated lotion on my thighs, wrap them in plastic, and run five miles. Try it some time. You'll have thin thighs, but you'll smell like Ben Gay the rest of your life."

"No, thanks." He studied her quietly, no humor softening the frown on his expressive face. "And you walked out a day before the Miss America Pageant. Pretty gutsy. I heard it had to do with your father's death."

Dinah stood and began clearing the table. Careful, now, she warned herself. Be casual, be cool. "My father had a little Cessna airplane that he loved to fly. He took it out one Saturday morning. Something went wrong, and he crashed. That happened just a few weeks before the pageant." She looked at Rucker helplessly. "I couldn't go on. The pageant was important to him, not to me."

Rucker frowned. What she'd done was like running away, as far as he was concerned, and something about it didn't add up. He never ran from anything or anybody, and he had the feeling that Dinah was the same way. "But wouldn't he have wanted you to hang in there?" Rucker asked. "I mean, you were a good bet to win. Wouldn't that have honored his memory more than throwing in the towel did?"

"No. Look, I'd rather not talk about my father, if you don't— "

"Well, yes, it would have," he persisted. "I mean, he wouldn't have wanted you to throw away all the hard work he did, and you did, and just run off, would he? He wanted you to be Miss America, and you should have—"

"Thank you for the hindsight critique," she interrupted in a tight, wounded voice. Standing with her hands full of dishes, Dinah glared down at him.

He gazed at her speculatively. "I've got a big mouth," he offered.

She wanted to tell him, but couldn't, that winning the pageant would have done no honor to her father if a sleazy tabloid reporter named Todd Norins had accomplished his goal, which was to dig up dirt on the new Miss America.

"I did what was right, believe me," she said hoarsely. "You're not one of those people who believes I had some sort of tawdry photos to hide, are you? Well, I don't."

But what she did have to hide was worse, in its way. Todd Norins had suspected that. Now he co-hosted a network gossip show called *USA Personal*. Dinah considered it a no-class rip-off of *60 Minutes*, and the thought that Norins might someday take an interest in her had given her nightmares over the years.

Rucker got up and took the dirty dishes from her. "You're one helluva woman, and I know you had good reasons for what you did. I didn't mean to make you feel bad." Dinah inhaled softly, unprepared for such sensitivity. Her eyes filled with tears. Rucker saw them and winced. "Don't, Dee," he said softly. "You've got all this old sadness in you. I see it. I'm sorry I—"

"No. I . . . I'm sorry," she said.

Looking distressed, he leaned forward and kissed her forehead. "If you cry, I swear I'll cry, too, and that's a disgusting sight. My nose runs and my eyes swell."

Soft laughter burst from her lips. "It's all right," she told him, and she touched his cheek affectionately. "Let's change the subject."

The slight devilish lift to his right eyebrow warned her that he was going to sidetrack this somber mood of theirs. "If you do have some naked pictures of yourself, I know a guy named Guido who could turn 'em into a real nice calendar." Dinah slapped his shoulder playfully. "We could make a lot of money—"

"Stop," she begged, chuckling. "Put the dishes in the sink and I'll get the champagne."

She played more Chopin on the piano while he sat beside her sipping his champagne from a fluted glass that looked absurdly delicate in his big hand. The fire crackled softly, and a single lamp surrounded the two of them with intimate shadows. Rucker was quiet and attentive. When she finished he nodded his approval. "Pretty," he said in a soft voice. "I like it. I could listen to it all night."

The suggestion concerned more than Chopin. Dinah put her hands in her lap and studied them pensively. They were trembling a little. "And then what?" she whispered.

She could feel his eyes on her as he carefully set his empty glass on the floor. He spoke to her just as carefully, as if she might break. "Then I'll bring you breakfast in bed. I can cook well enough to fry eggs and burn toast." He paused. "I'll find ways to keep you from noticin' the burned toast."

"I don't think one night could bridge our culture gap."

His leg was nearly touching hers. Affection and desire flowed from him in warm waves, and she knew that she returned it. His voice was a sensual rumble as he leaned closer and said, "I think one night would prove that we're perfect together."

"Or it could ruin an odd but enjoyable friendship."

"That's not really what worries you, Dee." He made that comment as a statement, not a question. Rucker slid an arm around her shoulders in a comforting way. "I'm not a dangerous man."

But he was dangerous, because newspaper columnists liked to ask probing questions. They also liked to write about the people in their personal lives, and she couldn't have that. "What worries you?" he whispered. "What makes you sit here shiverin' because you want me to hold you, but you don't want to do anything about it? This is right, Dee, very right. Talk to me, Dee. I've got to know what's wrong. Tell me—"

She stopped his upsetting interrogation with a kiss, then twisted her body to nestle tightly into the crook of his shoulder. She rested her hands against his chest, kneading the powerful muscles sheathed in his soft shirt. She caught roughly at that shirt, pressed herself close to him, and kissed him again, sliding her tongue into his mouth with aggressive passion.

The questions he'd had were lost in his amazement. His arms enclosed her in a hungry, breath-stealing embrace. He held her as if he were a desperate lover about to be separated from her forever, and he kissed her with a passion that sought to shove away the past and the future for a present that was sheer sensation.

"I want you," he told her. "More than I've ever wanted anyone."

Rucker drew her onto his lap and ran one exploring hand up the outside of her body from knee to breast. The slow, gripping journey of his fingers set off volcanoes of sensation under her skin, and when he cupped her soft, full breast in his palm she nearly cried from the exquisite care and concern in his touch.

His mustache had a delicious, coarse texture that tantalized her as he trailed his mouth down the smooth skin of her neck. At the base of her throat he sucked gently at the skin over her pulse. The sensation was incredible, and Dinah sank her hands into his thick hair and let her head drape back.

"Tonight," he murmured. "And after tonight." He put his lips against the flushed skin beneath her ear. His thumb found the ridge of her nipple under the sweater and rubbed it rhythmically. "I'll do anything for you, Dee. In bed, out of bed. Just give me a chance."

She cried out in bittersweet protest and, putting both palms against his shoulders, pushed firmly. He leaned back, and she looked down at him with sorrowful eyes. "We don't have enough in common," she begged in a hoarse voice. "It's all well and good to laugh about it, to tease each other, but you don't want to get involved with a woman who doesn't particularly like to cook, who doesn't like the same music or hobbies you like, who has a full-time career and intends to keep it."

"I want to be with you," he emphasized. "And nothing else is important but that." He looked at her with a sudden frown, his worried eyes showing how wounded he felt. "Do you really think I'm some sort of stupid, backward cretin who needs a harem girl?"

"No," she gasped, shocked. He was so hurt. Dinah shook her head fervently. "Oh, no, of course not. And I'm not some sort of elitist snob. But Rucker, there's too much . . . we're not compatible . . ."

"That's an excuse, not a reason," he said hoarsely. "You don't want to compromise. You don't want to take a chance. Dammit, this is a grand thing between us, a special thing, and I can't believe you don't want to admit it."

"I do admit it. I don't want to ruin it."

His hands gripped her arms. "We're not gonna ruin it."

She took a ragged breath, inhaling determination

with it. "That's right. Because we're not going to be anything but friends."

His hand slid slowly down the center of her sweater and paused over her left breast. Anger and sorrow were molded in his features. "Your heart's beatin'," he said, "but does it feel anything?"

She nodded and thought, It aches as if you were tearing it out. But she only told him, "I'm sorry."

"I pushed too hard, is that it? Too hard, too fast."

"No. I let you push. I didn't tell you how I felt because I didn't know how I felt. But I do now. I think you better leave."

One of his hands stayed on her arm as she moved off his lap and stood up. Dinah squeezed his shoulder, then forced her hand away from him before she gave into the urge to place her fingertips on his face and caress away all the bewilderment and sorrow she'd put there. "I'll get your jacket," she told him. He nodded and let his hand trail away from her.

When he stood at the door, the jacket in his hand, he looked down at her with a pensive frown, as if he were certain that he could understand her if he only studied her long enough.

Dinah cleared her throat and hoped that he couldn't tell how close she was to tears. "If you'd like to go back to Birmingham right away, I'll make your excuses about the pep rally tomorrow," she assured him.

"I don't run from problems, Dee," he said in a low, grim voice.

"So I'm a problem?" She smiled wistfully.

"No. A mystery. One I intend to unravel."

She gazed up at him with worried, searching eyes. "Is that the writer or the man speaking?" she asked.

"Both."

Dinah almost reached out to him then. Her hand rose but halted in midair. "There's nothing to know," she said.

Rucker's look said he didn't believe that in the least. He raised one hand to stroke her cheek. The sensual gesture was a warning that he knew at least one way to destroy her defenses if he had to.

"Good night," he said.

"Good night." Her stomach in knots, Dinah followed him onto the porch and stood at its edge, watching as he walked to his car. He turned, held up one hand in a final good night, and got in the car. She waited motionless in the chilly night air, hugging herself as the Cadillac disappeared down the long driveway toward the paved road.

Dinah continued to stand in the dark, her throat closed with restrained sorrow, her mind blank. Suddenly she was aware of a soft clicking sound, the sound of small feet scraping across old wood. Frightened, she hurried inside and flicked a switch. Light poured onto the porch from an overhead fixture, and Dinah caught her breath.

"Possum," she said tenderly, and knelt by the door as the rotund, ugly little creature waddled toward her. He stopped, sniffing the air suspiciously, and she knew that he was looking for Rucker, not her.

Dinah held out her hands to him, and eventually he came to her. Tears slid down her face as she picked him up. "You just couldn't leave that rascal alone, could you?" she said raggedly. "I don't know if I can either."

Four

"Pump it, Ms. Sheridan, pump it!"

"Go for the burn, the burn!"

Dinah exhaled a long, strenuous breath and curled the twenty-pound barbell up to her chest one last time. Then she grabbed it with both hands and lowered it gingerly back to its rack. She straightened the delicate mauve material of her chic, double-breasted suit dress and eyed the two students with a mildly baleful gaze. Eddie Burcher captained the wrestling team. Lorna Lancaster was ranked highly in state track and field events. They were both in disgustingly fine, teenaged condition, Dinah thought.

"I just came down to the weight room to ask a quick question about technique," she protested. "I'm an old woman who'll be thirty in just three years. What are you trying to do? Give a teacher heart palpitations?"

They laughed. "If you want to learn, you've got to suffer and sweat," Lorna told her. "We can't just tell you how to lift the weight. You have to practice."

"Suffering is beneath me," Dinah joked. "I'll work out devotedly, but I'll never forget what Cicero said: 'The pursuit, even of the best things, ought to be calm and tranquil.' "

"Cicero," Eddie echoed. "Didn't he play for the Rams?"

Dinah smothered a smile. "The Romans," she corrected drolly. "An Italian team that was big on philosophy."

"Oh," he grunted. "Well, we better go. We gotta get a good seat for the pep rally. See ya at the game tonight."

Dinah grimaced as she rubbed her aching arm. "Perk up, Ms. Sheridan," Lorna urged. "It's Friday afternoon. Class is over for the week."

"Go away. I'm old and out of shape. I've got no perk."

They laughed again, and she shooed them with a graceful wave of one hand. Dinah watched Eddie and Lorna stroll out of the weight room hand in hand. Love, Dinah thought pensively, can blossom even in the most unusual circumstances. But not with Rucker McClure, she added. Alone among the cool, concrete-block walls, she let sorrow and concern settle inside her again. She walked wearily to an ancient soft-drink machine in one corner.

Her small mauve purse lay atop her briefcase on a weight bench nearby. Dinah retrieved some change and put it in the machine, which rattled, hummed, and produced absolutely nothing in the way of a canned drink.

Dinah jiggled the coin return. No response. She put in more money. The machine ate it. Dinah's eyes narrowed. She hadn't slept well after last night's disturbing dinner with Rucker. She wasn't in the mood to be flamboozled by a mechanical monster. " 'These violent delights have violent ends,' " she muttered. "So sayeth Shakespeare." Then she raised a fist and whacked the machine hard.

"Let's hear some applause for the Mount Pleasant Masher and the Killer Soda Machine!" an unmistakable voice boomed behind her. "This rasslin' match is one fall and a ten-minute TV time limit!"

Dinah whirled around to find Rucker leaning against the door to the weight room, his arms crossed over his chest. In honor of the pep rally he had on his speech suit: the boots, corduroys, houndstooth jacket, white shirt, and brown tie. A slight smile tugged at the corner of his mustache, but his eyes looked tired.

Flustered, Dinah said nothing for a moment. Then she pointed to the soft-drink dispenser. "I suppose, seeing as how you're a macho man and all such men have innate mechanical ability, that you can retrieve the can that seems to be stuck in this thing's craw?"

He nodded and walked toward her, smoothly side-stepping weight equipment, his stride easy and his body twisting in a confident, athletic way that riveted her eyes to the movements. Unanswered questions and emotion seemed to thicken the air as he stopped in front of her, his eyes intense.

"So you need a real man," he said smugly. The smile hinted around his mouth again, belying the awkwardness between them. "Admit it."

"I need a sledge hammer." She bit her lower lip to keep from smiling back at him. "You're a good substitute."

He grasped his chest dramatically. "That's no way to get what you want. Didn't they teach you anything in those beauty parades? Like how to be sweet and simperin' when you need something from a man?"

Dinah batted her eyelashes and looked up at him coyly. He provoked absurdity and silliness. She loved it and was glad they could still joke after last night's unhappy discussion. "You big, strong, masculine toad, won't you please help helpless, itsy-bitsy me?"

"Of course, little lady." He squatted beside the machine and jabbed his hand under the metal flap that covered the dispenser opening. While he fiddled and felt, she studied him.

"What can I do for you today?" she asked.

He tugged his jacket sleeve back and wiggled his hand higher into the machine. A look of amused distaste crossed his face. "This reminds me of the time I went over to my cousin Lucy's farm and the vet was payin' a house call to an expectant cow."

Dinah burst into soft laughter and he looked up, smiling under troubled eyes. "I like it when you laugh," he told her. "I don't like upsettin' you." He paused. "Like last night."

"Oh, Rucker." Her heart aching, she knelt beside him on the room's stained green carpet. "I don't like upsetting you either. I didn't enjoy that."

He paused in his assault on the soda machine, his hand still inside its metal maze, to look at her with bittersweet yearning. "Will you sit beside me at the pep rally?" he asked in a mock-shy tone. "I'm scared to be around all these teenage girls alone. They have a lot of hormones and they like mature men."

"Then you have nothing to worry about," she assured him dryly. "Oh. By the way, your possum came back. If you want him—"

"My baby!" he exclaimed gleefully, grinning. "My little dumpling wants to stay with its daddy? I never thought—" The machine emitted an ominous metallic click. "What the . . ." Rucker's grin faded as he tried to pull his hand out of the dispenser opening. "Aw, come on, this is ridiculous." He pulled harder.

Dinah's eyes widened in alarm. "Are you stuck?"

"Nah. When I was a juvenile delinquent I used to rig these machines and . . . dammit!"

"You're stuck," she confirmed.

He looked at her with a deadpan expression. "I'm stuck."

Dinah sat down on the floor, tucking her feet, in their mauve pumps, under her. He sat down, too, awkwardly, then leaned his shoulder against the machine. He crooked one leg under him and drew the other up so that he could rest his free arm on it with at least a degree of jaunty aplomb. She lifted the dispenser door and slid her hand inside, contacting Rucker's large muscular wrist.

"Let me see." She slid her fingers up his wrist to the imprisoned hand. "I might be able to help."

"It's hopeless," he said wistfully. "Don't be brave."

"You're trapped between two cans and the rack that holds them. Oh, Rucker, I better go get the janitor."

"I don't need to be mopped or swept. I need to be rescued."

She began to laugh. "Some macho man!"

He frowned in grand fashion. "Even John Wayne, God rest his fine soul, couldn't have conquered this damned sneaky machine!"

"I wish I had a camera! I wonder how many magazines and newspapers would love to have a photograph of Rucker McClure being eaten by a soda machine!"

"Aw, Dee, you mean thing."

She laughed harder. Dinah clasped his shoulders

and leaned forward, unconcerned that she was cackling like a deranged hen. Through years of beauty competitions she'd been rigidly trained to modulate her voice and her laughter. Now that training deserted her, but oddly she didn't mind. She made boisterous squeaking sounds and rested her forehead against his shoulder. No other man in the world could provoke me this way, she thought suddenly.

"You're . . . in-incredible!" she yelped. "Fantas . . . tic!"

"Well, howdy do," he retorted dryly. "Women get turned on by the strangest things." Then his free arm swept around her waist. Shocked into silence and gulping for breath, Dinah tilted her head back and stared at him warily. "Forget the janitor. Stay here and console me," he ordered. His voice dropped languidly. "The least you can do is give a prisoner a little entertainment."

Her lips were parted in surprise when his mouth covered them. Without thinking, Dinah made a soft, grateful sound. He echoed it in gruff harmony and twisted his mouth on hers with slow, erotic intent. Several long seconds passed as indecision warred with affection and desire. Finally Dinah sighed in defeat. I can't resist a man trapped in a soft-drink machine, she thought raggedly. It's not fair. She slipped her arms around his neck and kissed him back, darting her tongue into his mouth to taste and excite, brushing her lips over his mustache, nuzzling the delightfully coarse skin of his cheek.

"You were just scared last night," he told her. "You know we ought to be together. This proves it."

"Oh, Rucker, it doesn't prove a thing," she whispered. "Except that you need someone to protect you from vicious soda machines. You appeal to my nurturing instincts."

"I'm takin' applications for a body guard," he said hoarsely. "You just got the job." He kissed her hard, and his hand slid around to the front of her dress. Dinah gasped against his mouth as she pushed his hand away.

"Rucker, I would never do anything . . . in the school weight room," she protested firmly.

"Everyone's gone to get ready for the pep rally," he countered. He grasped her hand and they shared a look full of intimate communication. "Be just a little wild, Madam Mayor," he drawled in a sensual tone. His eyes taunted her to relax. "I'm trapped in the dad-blasted soft-drink machine. I can't be too much of a threat." He wiggled his captured arm and grimaced.

Dinah's breath punctuated the still air with soft, raspy sounds. "We're not compatible . . ."

"Then we'll just be having a little meaningless fun, won't we?"

He cupped her breast through the fabric of her dress. "Now that," he whispered, his face close to hers, "feels like an A-plus beautiful bosom, teacher."

Shivering, Dinah buried her face against his neck and clutched his coat collar. "It's been a long time," she said in a voice that vibrated with emotion.

"Since a man touched you? I'm glad." His thumb flicked back and forth, igniting exquisite pinpoints of excitement. "This is so special. We're special together."

"It won't work between us, Rucker."

"Tell me why. Tell me those secrets you keep bottled up."

"No secrets," she said too quickly.

"Ssssh. Whatever they are, they don't matter to me." He began kissing her neck. "My proper, elegant beauty queen," he whispered into her ear with teasing rebuke. "I'm just a rowdy dirt-dauber from the wrong side of the tracks, and I don't know how to be proper. Or elegant. All I know is that I'm fallin' in love with you and I want you to fall in love with me."

Dinah pulled away from him, conscious of where they were, even though the school was deserted. The teacher in her came to the fore. "I can't. . . . I can't. . . ." she pleaded.

"You can't at least admit that you want to make love with me?" He took hold of her hand. "That's the simple part, Dee. The physical want is the simple part. I know we've got no problem there."

"But everything else . . ."

"Would work itself out." He pulled her close again

and placed slow, damp kisses along her collar bone.
Dinah closed her eyes, caught up in the wonderful
sensations of his mouth. "You want me, Dee," he
challenged softly, his breath ragged.

Dinah felt as if reality had deserted her. Her emotions, her needs, her soul were being drawn out of her
by the man whose mouth continued to tantalize her.
"I've never been irresponsible," she murmured. "Kissing in public! In the weight room! Oh, oh, your
mustache . . ."

"Like it?" he asked.

"Like it," she answered in trembling tones.

"Your skin smells like tea roses," he murmured. "And
you taste like sweet cream."

They leaned as one against the soft-drink machine,
and Dinah's head draped back. She closed her eyes and
lost track of time as he nuzzled her. Dinah couldn't
help smiling. She was beyond regret.

The soft-drink machine clicked and rattled. Rucker's
head came up and Dinah opened her eyes groggily.
They shared a look of speculation. "It turned you loose,"
she said between short breaths. "You're free. We can
get up now."

"No, no. I'm still trapped." He shook his head fervently, trying in vain to look sincere. She chuckled.
The pleasure in his eyes was a potent aphrodisiac.
"Oh, Dee," he said in a low, vibrant voice. Then he slid
his arm around her waist again. "Kiss me one more
time," he whispered. "Then I'll let you go."

It was a slow, chaste kiss, and yet it left her shivering with more desire than ever. "That's enough," she
said desperately. "Please. I want to stop."

His hand slid out of the drink machine. It held a can.
His eyes tempting and amused, he pressed the icy
metal lip to her shoulder and traced a dewy line down
to her collar. He popped the can open and held it out,
smiling knowingly. "Bet you never expected a soft drink
to bring you so much excitement," he quipped. He
glanced at it. "Decaffeinated, even."

Smiling weakly, Dinah took the can. She was too
drained to resist what he suggested next, and he knew

it. "Sit with me at the pep rally," he coaxed. She nodded. "Have dinner with me." She nodded again. "Sit with me at the football game tonight." She nodded a third time. "And then . . ."

"Stop while you're ahead," she warned softly. The man might think he'd settled all her doubts and left her ripe for seduction, but he was wrong. A slow, patient smile curved his mouth.

"I'm ahead," he agreed. "So I'll stop. For right now, at least."

Wally Oscar was president of the Mount Pleasant Chamber of Commerce. He owned a combination country-antiques shop and gas station on the outskirts of town, and therefore catered successfully to hordes of tourist traffic. He had a shock of white hair that, due to some law of physics which Dinah had never fully analyzed, stood up in odd little tufts. Wally Oscar always looked as though he'd been recently electrified, she thought.

"That's a danged good one!" he bellowed as the Mount Pleasant Wildcats made a first down. He jumped up, then plopped down. His knitted scarf fell off his squat little neck.

"A danged good one!" Rucker echoed. Dinah watched in rapt amusement as the two men turned to each other and shook hands.

"Want another snootful?" Wally asked slyly. He gestured with one gloved hand toward the thermos bottle stationed between his loafers.

Dinah smiled puckishly as Rucker twisted his head and caught her eye. His expression contained a gentlemanly question. "I don't mind," she assured him. "I just don't understand how you can bear to drink grain alcohol mixed with coffee."

"It's a real man's drink. In college, we called it a ball—well, uh, a real masculine name." His breath came out frosty in the cold night air. Under the colorful stadium blanket that they shared, his big hand squeezed her fingers possessively. They smiled at each other.

"Go ahead and have another 'snootful,' " she told him. "I'm glad you're having a good time, like a real man."

She was having a good time too. The night was clear and crisp, the game was going in the Wildcats' favor, the bleachers were full of happy, nosy townspeople who kept winking at her, and the man beside her made no secret of the fact that he treasured her company. She knew this moment couldn't last, that she and Rucker McClure couldn't last, but she refused to think about that right now.

Wally plunked a set of radio earphones on his head and began humming to himself. Rucker edged closer to her so that their legs touched from hip to knee. He rubbed his knee against hers. "You look great in those blue corduroy pants," he told her. "I'm glad you changed clothes. I liked your purple dress, but I like pants better. Especially with that nice sweater." He peered in admiration at the white, ribbed-neck sweater that peeked between the halves of her leather coat. Dinah smiled. She suspected that he liked the sweater because it was snug, but he wasn't going to say so in public.

"My dress, sir, was mauve."

"Nah. Light purple. Don't be prissy."

Dinah huffed in mild rebuke but didn't argue with him further. They'd developed a light, perfectly pleasant and perfectly safe camaraderie since the soda machine incident, and she wanted to preserve the mood. He'd gone back to the motel to change into jeans, a bulky Auburn University sweatshirt, a creaky, brown aviator's jacket, and his jogging shoes. He'd picked her up at her house and they'd eaten dinner at a family-style restaurant, where they talked amiably over plates of fresh fish, steaming vegetables, and fluffy biscuits.

He told her that he didn't care for astrology, TV weathermen, computers, dentists, and getting up early in the morning. She agreed with him on astrology and dentists but said she loved computers and could tolerate the rest. He kept bringing up little things people in town had mentioned to him about her—how quiet she'd been when she first moved there and how puzzled everyone was that she wanted to build a life in such a tiny place.

Dinah tactfully sidestepped his attempts to learn what lay in her past. She told him the neutral facts—that her father had been president of one of Georgia's largest banks, that she'd had a privileged, happy childhood, though she'd been shy, bookish, too tall, and ungainly. He'd never been shy or bookish, but he had been too tall and, in his words, "thinner than cheap spaghetti," so they talked about those things.

And now he sat here perfectly at home, as he seemed to be wherever he went, glorying in the night and the game and her presence, singing along as the Wildcat band belted out a pop tune, and she wanted to hug him tightly without ever letting him go. "You know," he told her after the band finished, "I'd forgotten how wonderful a small-town football game could be." He glanced at Wally, found him still preoccupied with his radio, and handed his cup of doctored coffee to Dinah. "Get rid of it diplomatically, Dee," he urged in a whisper. "It's awful. It always was. I'm old enough to admit that now without bein' embarrassed."

"Another real man bites the dust." She nearly sputtered with laughter as she sat the cup down by one of her high-heeled leather boots. Casually she let her toe tip it over so that the contents cascaded toward the grassy earth far beneath the metal stadium benches. "Good work," Rucker praised as she handed the empty cup to him. His other hand, the one under the blanket, curled tighter around hers. He looked down at her in a way that made cozy pleasure wind around her rib cage. "You make me remember how much fun life used to be," he told her solemnly. "Before I got a lot of money and moved into a yuppie house with yuppie neighbors. Before I lost my roots."

"Rucker," she teased gently, "you may have a long vine, but your roots are always evident. Believe me."

He chuckled. "How do you know whether I have a long vine or not?" he asked coyly. "Want to find out?"

Dinah made a garbled sound as she analyzed what she'd said. "No comment," she muttered.

"Well," he drawled in smug, comical satisfaction, thrusting his chest forward, "I'll take that as a *maybe*."

Dinah pretended to watch the game, while her mind churned over decisions. She had no clear-cut answers about him anymore, only disturbing *maybe*'s that brought no sense of security. Maybe if she told him the truth about the scandal that still lurked in her background, he'd keep it confidential. But maybe he wouldn't. Maybe he was as wonderful as he seemed, or maybe he was a glib con artist like that other reporter, Todd Norins. Maybe he'd bring something wonderful into her life. Or maybe he'd bring disaster. Her good mood began to evaporate.

On the way to his car after the game he was approached by one person after another who wanted his autograph. Dinah watched with brooding intensity as he signed football programs, paper cups, and napkins, trying to come to a decision about him. Several women kissed him, and some made no attempt to hide the gleam of invitation in their eyes. Dinah was amazed to find herself squinting at them in a predatory assessment. This jealousy is a very bad sign, she thought anxiously. I have to nip it in the bud.

"I didn't smooch those gals back, you noticed," he pointed out proudly when they were seated in the Cadillac.

Dinah made sure her answer sounded confident and blithe. "You should have. You're a likable rowdy with an eye for the ladies. It doesn't bother me in the least. The public loves it."

"Hmmm." He looked at her shrewdly. "I smell an insinuation."

Dinah spent a long time arranging her stadium cushion, purse, and blanket. "Why should I feel possessive toward you? I'm a very secure person, and besides, we've only known each other a few days. We don't have any kind of understanding."

He turned to face her, planting one big hand on the back of the car seat and one on the dashboard. It was an aggressive posture, and Dinah's pulse increased nervously. Even in the dim light of a street lamp she saw the sudden anger in his eyes. "What the hell was all *that* supposed to mean?" he demanded. "Don't dilly-dally with me, Madam Mayor. Spit it out."

"I just want things to be clear between us before we get back to my house." Dinah kept her voice very neutral. "There isn't going to be a repeat of the infamous weight-room scene. There isn't going to be anything at all."

He was lethally silent for a moment. "What happened?" he asked in a low, tense voice. "What rule did I break in the past hour that changed your attitude toward me?"

"No rule," she answered, forcing her voice to remain calm. "My attitude's no different now than it was before." She took a steadying breath. "I was caught off guard this afternoon. We had a nice time tonight. But that's as far as it goes. You're a journalist. I'm a politician. That combination can't be anything but unstable. Plus, we come from different backgrounds. We don't like the same music, the same food, the same television shows, the same books—"

"Dee," he interrupted, his voice deadly soft, "you're a damned snob."

"No!" She shook her head fiercely. "Don't you dare accuse me of that! It's not true!"

"The hell it's not. I see it now, plain as day." He faced forward, cranked the Cadillac's engine, and slammed it into gear. "I've got no use for your elitist arrogance."

Dinah was so stunned by his elegant choice of words that she stared at him in silence as he whipped the car out of its spot in the teacher's parking lot. An odd sense of awe swelled her chest. Don't ever underestimate the depth and power of this man's intellect, she warned herself. She shook her head angrily, frustrated by his unfair accusation and all too aware that she'd hurt him. He pointed the car toward an exit.

"Rucker, would you please drive around behind the school?" she asked tensely. "I have patrol duty this week, which means I play warden to students who are back there drinking beer. I'm sorry, but I have to check before we leave."

"Fine," he retorted. He swung the car to the left and followed the parking lot as it curved around one end of the school building. Hardly able to concentrate, Dinah hurriedly scanned the dark nooks and crannies. The back of the building was etched in angular shadows from the street lights.

"Stop," she ordered abruptly. He jammed on the brakes as they passed an L-shaped indentation in the old structure. "What in the world? Those aren't students!"

They saw a disturbing tableau. Three good-sized young men had cornered a fourth. The three aggressors were surprisingly respectable looking in jeans and jackets; the fourth man, who had his fists raised in a boxer's defensive pose, wore a Marine uniform. "The Peevy brothers!" Dinah exclaimed. "They run a feed store in Bartley. And they love to fight. Damn their Neanderthal hides."

Rucker put the car in park and sat staring at the scene for a moment, his chest rising and falling erratically. The Peevys turned around and glowered. One of them gestured with a curt movement of his hand, indicating clearly that the Cadillac should go back where it came from.

Dinah thumped the car seat angrily. "Let's go. I'll get Dewey to come break this up."

Without turning to look at her, his voice deep and stern, Rucker said, "They'll beat the tar out of that Marine before Dewey gets here."

He reached for the door handle and Dinah grabbed his arm. "No!"

Rucker turned to look at her then. His expression was set, his gaze somber. "We rednecks have our pride," he told her tautly. "We believe in fair fights. And we don't let a bunch of bastards dishonor a man in uniform." He paused. "But you wouldn't understand any of that."

"Rucker!" Amazed and upset, she held onto his jacket sleeve. He firmly pried her fingers off it and got out of the car. "If you hit anyone, I'll never forgive you!" she called desperately just as he slammed the door shut.

Five

"Sit down and don't move! If you do, I'll . . . I'll . . ."

"Calm down, Dee," Rucker said in a careful, soothing tone. He walked through her living room to the old hearth, sat down on it, and gingerly balanced his hands on his denimed knees. He was well aware that the moonlit room was a cocoon filled with Dinah's gestating anger. She flung her leather coat on an upholstered armchair.

"Don't tell me to calm down, you ruffian! Not after what you just put me through!" Dinah didn't care if her voice was strained and shaky. She snapped on a floor lamp near the fireplace and stomped into her kitchen. *"Bonjour!"* Nureyev called from his perch by the window. Dinah clicked on a soft light over the sink.

"Pipe down!" she told the crow as she grabbed a large mixing bowl from a bottom cabinet. She'd never before been involved in an escapade like tonight's. Rucker had punched one Peevy in the jaw and another in the ribs. The third Peevy had battled unsuccessfully with the Marine. Dinah slammed the bowl into the sink then rubbed her temples, trying to unscramble her emotions. The fight had been terrifying and brutal but also, she had to admit, wildly exciting. She was furious at Rucker for brawling and mad at herself for feeling so primitively thrilled.

Her teeth clenched so hard that her jaw ached, Dinah filled the mixing bowl with warm water and carried it back to the living room. Rucker bent forward, crooning to his possum, which had waddled out from its sleeping place in her guest bedroom. It squatted, an ugly gray oddity on her creamy carpet, between his feet. "Here," Dinah ordered. Her arms trembling, she sloshed water out as she plunked the bowl down on the hearth. "Put your hands in that."

He looked up at her solemnly but couldn't resist lifting a jaunty auburn brow. "How 'bout I put my head in it and drown? Wouldn't you like that better?"

"Don't push me, 'Charles Bronson' McClure." Her voice was so unsteady that she had to stop for a deep breath. "Don't even talk to me."

She continued her business in icy silence, knowing that his worried green eyes tracked every move she made. She threw logs onto the hearth grate and quickly started a fire. Then she marched to her bathroom at the back of the house and brought back a washcloth, bandages, and antiseptic ointment. She sat down beside him and unceremoniously grabbed one of his hands out of the bowl.

"Ouch," he deadpanned. "You're bein' mean."

"Shut up," she said, and her voice broke. Tears slid over her dark lashes and down her cheeks. Crying softly, she kept her eyes trained on her ministrations to his bruised, scraped knuckles. An anguished part of her wanted to croon sweet things to those knuckles, but she firmly ignored the urge.

"Oh, Dee," he said gruffly. "Dee, don't cry." He reached out with his other hand to smooth back a strand of dark hair that clung to her wet face, but she raised her eyes and glared a warning at him.

"You brawling maniac," she said. "Don't touch me. Put that hand back! Put it back in the water! Don't drip on my carpet!"

He obeyed slowly. "I embarrassed you," he told her in a weary voice. "I reckon the kind of man you admire would have had more dignity than to fight. He would have gone for the police, or sweet-talked those pig kissers into calling it a night." He glanced down at his torn sweatshirt and dirt-stained jeans. "But I had to help that Marine out. He was just a kid."

Remembering his earlier accusation about her attitude, she shook her fist at him and choked back sobs. "You d-did not embarrass me! I'm not an elitist, arrogant snob! Be quiet!"

"At least those Peevy boys'll think twice before they gang up on anybody else. And you said they don't even live in Mount Pleasant. It's not like you have to worry about losin' their votes."

"I don't care about the Peevys! I'm upset at *you*! I've never"—she brushed at her face roughly—"never seen such a wanton, reckless display of self-gratifying egotism in my entire life! A grown man who can't solve problems without using his fists! A man who's willing to risk being maimed or killed for the sake of some macho code of honor! Rambo!"

"And what's wrong with Rambo?" he asked angrily. He jerked his hand away from her. "Dammit, I may have embarrassed you, but you get down off your high horse and give me some respect!"

She grabbed his hand back. "You . . . did . . . not . . . embarrass . . . me!" she emphasized between clenched teeth.

"What, then?" he demanded fiercely.

"I was proud of you, you idiot!" She clutched his hand, and her head drooped over it as she tried to hide the new tears that cascaded down her face.

After a shocked moment he whispered in an incredulous voice, "You were? Then why are you mad as a wet settin' hen?"

"Because you could have gotten your thick skull cracked! You frightened me and I hate feeling frightened! I don't know what I'm going to do with you! Or about you! I want a predictable, cerebral, sophisticated man; a diplomatic—"

"A wimp," he intoned.

"Ooooh," she moaned in disgust. Why did she care about this man even more now than before? Damn his appeal and his way of making her feel exquisitely female. Dinah smeared the back of his hand with ointment. "Just quit talking, Rucker. Just let me finish this in peace!"

He complied gallantly, and when both his hands were bandaged he got up without a word and took the bowl of water back to the kitchen. Dinah propped her head on one hand and stared into the fire, trying to reclaim her good sense. But one important fact was undeniable. She was proud of Rucker. Deeply proud.

"Here, nurse." She looked up to find him holding out a tumbler half full of brandy. Dinah took it as he sat down on the hearth, facing her. He had a similar glass in his hand. He reached over and clinked it to hers. "To regrets." He paused, his eyes troubled.

She gazed at him in tearful puzzlement. "Regrets?"

He nodded, and suddenly she noticed how weary and dejected he looked. He took a deep swallow of brandy and stared into the fire. "I'll be goin' back to Birmingham tomorrow."

Dinah opened her mouth in dismay. A thousand new conflicts battled inside her. Going? He was going? "Why?" she asked in a small voice.

He studied her with disarming intensity. "Because it's for the best."

"Who's best?" she blurted. "Your best, or mine? What do you know about what's best for anyone?"

A frown began to pull his expressive brows together. "Dammit, don't fiddle-faddle around with words. You want me outta here, I'm going."

Dinah stared at him for several seconds, her lips parted, her mind churning. Then she stood and walked quickly to a pair of windows that looked out on the back porch and the woods beyond it. She sat her brandy on the white bookshelf beside the windows and leaned one hand on the sleek wood, then she gazed blankly into the darkness outside. You can't let him go, a wise inner voice told her. It's foolish to keep him here, she countered.

Her body stiffened as Rucker stopped behind her. He clasped her shoulders firmly, his fingers communicating the dangerous sensuality that had simmered between them since the night they met. Dinah shivered and shut her eyes, feeling the size and heat of his body as if he were pressing against her back.

"Say it," he urged hoarsely. "Just say, 'You don't have a snowball's chance in hell with me, Rucker,' and I'll leave."

Dinah took a deep breath and held tightly to the bookcase. "You don't have . . ." She stopped, her heart racing so fast that she felt dizzy. "You don't . . ." she tried again. She felt his hands trembling on her arms and realized with a bittersweet thrill that she had the power to make him happy or miserable. He held the same power over her. It's no good to be practical or logical about this man, she admitted suddenly. I'm crazy about him. Dinah twisted around, her eyes tormented. "Stay," she whispered raggedly.

"Oh, Dee."

The air was heavy with intoxicating promise. His eyes glowing with pleasure, he raised his battered hands and cupped her face. His fingertips roamed over the flushed skin, rubbing away the tear streaks, soothing the silky, swollen areas under her eyes. Dinah heard herself murmur incoherently. Then she slipped her arms around his neck and buried her fingers deep into his thick hair.

"Stay," she repeated in anguish. "But don't scare me with any more Rambo heroics. How do your hands feel?"

"What hands?" he teased. They roamed down to her arms, then dropped lower and clasped her waist, squeezing gently, pulling her forward. "Oh. These hands. They feel fine, darlin', just fine. I don't think they've ever had a better time."

Dinah closed her eyes and rested her forehead against his cheek. She felt his fingers slide down her lower back to her hips and, without the slightest inhibition, spread across her rump. There's nothing timid about this man, Dinah acknowledged with shocked pleasure. He caressed her with a lusty appreciation that was both good-hearted and blatantly seductive. Even through the thick corduroy of her slacks his technique worked its desired goal on her defenses. She groaned a little and curled against his body.

"There's a pure wildcat under your pretty pink skin, Madam Mayor," he taunted in a wicked, throaty voice.

"Temporary insanity. I've never—"

"Acted so . . . so un-mayorly before," he finished drolly. "I know." Rucker's voice dropped, becoming a thick murmur against her ear. "But, oh, little lady, you're gonna surprise yourself a whole lot more than this, before I'm through."

He curved his hands under her rump and abruptly picked her up. Dinah gripped his shoulders as he pressed her to the wall by the bookshelves. Suddenly his body was wedged between her legs, snug against her, and her thighs clung to his hips. Even though he was lean, he was a big man, and she cried out with the sensation of being overwhelmed. Quickly he adjusted his hold on her hips, making her more comfortable, cradling her gently.

"All right?" he asked in a worried, low voice. "Too rough?"

"No." She rested her head in the crook of his neck, and her voice was muffled against his warm skin. "I'm just feeling particularly female at this moment." She didn't tell him that this particularly dignified and pristine female had no idea how to deal with such an aggressive, bluntly sexual male. Men had always catered to her icy decorum and been careful not to ruffle her reserve. Not Rucker. He ruffled her reserve and everything else.

His tone was tender and amused. "I'll take that as a compliment, thank you, ma'am."

"It is, macho man, it is."

"You Jane, me Tarzan."

"You Rambo, me—I don't know what I am." She sounded resigned.

He spoke against her ear, his voice provocative and serious. "You're a prim little ol' beauty queen who's come to her senses."

Dinah slowly turned her face upwards and kissed his cheek. "I've lost my senses," she corrected.

"Same difference. You need to run wild a little." She moaned a soft, encouraging sound as he pushed his lower body further into the harbor of her thighs. "Come on, Dee," he murmured. "Run wild with me."

His very hard arousal was evident under the denim of his jeans, and when it found a home in the indentation of her body she welcomed it with a compliant movement of her hips. The wall was hard against her back; Rucker's body was almost as hard against her breasts and stomach. Suddenly she kissed him, grinding her mouth onto his with rough need.

He groaned in the back of his throat and rolled her gently from side to side, working his hips even tighter against her, pressing and releasing, showing her how good it would be if there were no clothes between them. Dinah gasped for air and retreated, smacking funny little kisses over his face in an attempt to playfully lighten the intense mood. Smiling weakly, he turned his face at various angles to catch every one.

"Hot damn," he said in a strangled voice. "This oughta be the national sport. Free-form smoochin'."

Dinah considered herself an efficient, responsible decision maker, and always had. Once a conclusion was reached, she didn't brood about the consequences, and tonight was no different. Dinah made her choice, and that choice was to take Rucker McClure into her life, her soul, and her bed.

"Carry me to my briefcase," she whispered, her mouth grazing his right ear. He pulled back, bewildered, and looked at her askance. "Over there on the couch," she added. "You'll see."

Still puzzled, he carried her to the plush white couch in front of the fireplace and sat down with her on his lap. She curled her legs on either side of him in a kneeling position, then reached for the sleek leather briefcase propped against one of the couch's arms.

"If you start gradin' history papers, I'm gonna dump you on the floor," Rucker threatened mildly.

Dinah could feel the color rising in her face as she flipped the latch. "No," she said softly, "it's not that." She reached inside the briefcase and felt around hurriedly, her pulse pounding harder with every second. When she withdrew her hand, she watched him look down at it curiously. His eyes widened and he exhaled with a rough sound. He put his hand out, palm up, and she deposited her gift with great care. Their gazes met.

"Are you sure, Dee?" he asked in a gruff tone.

Dinah cleared her throat delicately. "We had a sex education seminar for the seniors last week. These were leftovers." She paused, sounding almost defensive. "Someone had to take them home. The biology teacher didn't want them."

Sensual tension was a magnet that kept their eyes locked. "Are you sure, Dee?" he repeated.

Her chin came up proudly. "Yes."

He kissed her thoroughly and slowly, twisting his mouth against hers in a way that was both rough and tender. "I'll take the plain ones," he whispered, nodding toward the items he clenched in his fist. "The pink ones look sissy and the purple ones would make me feel like a carnival ride."

Dinah looked at him plaintively. "This is very difficult for me, admitting that I want you . . . want you to stay." She paused, her heart pounding. "That I want you."

His eyes were full of urgency as they searched her face. "I'll make it easier, Dee."

He swiftly rearranged her body so that he held her in his arms. Then he stood up, lifting her, and covered her mouth with another hungry, demanding kiss. The night shrank to nothing but the two of them, the nearness of two overwrought bodies, the communication of blue eyes and green, the silent, tender messages that flowed between them. He started toward the back of the house, his stride quick.

This is the right thing to do, she thought with one last shred of clear thought. I won't have any regrets.

He walked into her darkened bedroom and paused, getting his bearings amid the sleek contemporary furniture. Moonlight angled across the queen-size bed by the far wall, illuminating its satiny gray coverlet. The air was fragrant with the mingled scents of feminine colognes and the spicey pine burning in the living room fireplace. He went to the bed and laid her down in the moonlight, then stood looking down at her, breathing heavily. Dinah stretched out slowly, feminine instinct guiding her movements to be languid and inviting. Even in the dark she knew that his unwavering gaze mapped everything she did.

"Come here," she whispered.

"I don't take orders from women."

"I see." Dinah smiled, sensing the erotic game he wanted to play. "Pull your shirt off," she commanded. "*That's* an order."

"Make me, beauty queen."

She leaped up, her hands quivering, and wrestled his sweatshirt over his head. He fought with feigned resistance and lost gamely, then watched as she slung the garment onto the floor and climbed back onto the bed.

Dinah lay on her back again and felt her breath aching for passage. She swept her eyes over his magnificent chest covered in dark, thick hair. He carried a lot of his weight in that chest and the broad shoulders above it, but he was well proportioned. She watched a muscle quiver in the flat terrain at the edge of his jeans.

"Undress for me, Dee," he drawled in a tone as languorous as warm whiskey. "And then I'll undress for you."

Her body flooded with anticipation and surprise. Making love was supposed to be a politely orchestrated event, she had always thought, performed with the utmost delicacy and restraint. But neither delicacy nor restraint had a part in what was happening between her and Rucker.

"All right," she answered.

"Do it slow."

Pleasure shot through her at that sensual command. She began to comply, her eyes never leaving his shadowed face. "You're beautiful," he murmured. Then seconds later, "High-topped panties. You're sweet." And then, drawing out the words with an audible sigh of pleasure, "I knew that would be a fantastic bosom."

When she was naked, she put her arms behind her on the pillow. He was a dark, mysterious, and compelling shadow above her, a shadow that bent suddenly and grasped her ankles with big, calloused hands. She jumped, startled. "Easy, easy," he cajoled. His hands slid lightly up her legs, molding themselves to the curves. By the time he reached the smooth joining of thighs to hips, she could barely keep from writhing. His fingertips swirled deeply into the patch of dark, curly hair at the top of her thighs, then parted her legs and sought the moist, hot folds there. Dinah moaned and closed her eyes.

"It's not a great deal of fun being naked alone," she teased in a barely audible voice.

"You won't be alone in a second."

He moved away. Dinah opened her eyes and watched him strip off his shoes, socks, and jeans. "Plain BVD's," she commented, mimicking his earlier perusal of her underwear. "How sweet."

"I get no respect," he said playfully. Rucker removed them in quick, fluid motions, then stood naked before her, his hands by his sides, his chest moving with deep contractions.

After a moment of rapt study, Dinah whispered in a tender voice, "Oh, Rucker, you've got my respect."

What little restraint there was between them disappeared in a bonfire of passion as he came to the bed and lowered his body onto hers. Dinah twisted, loving the delicious sensation of his weight pressing her down and the feel of him naked. They kissed with fierce, hurried motions, again and again, while her hands feathered over his back like butterflies, lighting atop the powerful, flexing muscles there.

He groaned and grasped one of her hands gently, then rolled off her and lay on his back. "Dee, take care of me, so we'll be safe." Puzzled, Dinah watched as he fumbled for something on the far side of the bedspread. Then she realized that he was retrieving one of the small packages that he'd dropped on the bedspread when he put her down earlier.

Affection and tenderness filled her until she thought

she could rise and float on the moonlight. For all his blustery chauvinism and macho rowdiness, he was the best kind of man, because his words made it clear that she wasn't alone in this important responsibility. She took the package from him, then bent over his body and trailed damp, adoring kisses across his stomach. "That's not the kind of takin' care I meant," he protested in a gasping voice, as his back arched.

"I'll get to the point eventually," she promised.

"The point's ready."

She laughed weakly. Several minutes passed before she let him grab her in an impatient, trembling embrace. He slid a hand between her legs and stroked her expertly until she sagged against him, her fingers convulsing in his chest hair. "You shouldn't la-di-da with me," he said, smiling into the kiss she gave him. "I won't put up with it."

But suddenly she was beyond teasing. "Rucker," she whispered in a tiny voice. "Rucker, please."

His smile faded and he rolled her onto her back quickly, then nestled himself between her thighs. "Dee, this is the beginning of something wonderful," he whispered hoarsely.

"Something . . . wonderful," she agreed in a dazed tone, her head thrown back and eyes closed in bliss. She gasped as the turgid, smooth length of him slid inside her.

And then there was no more need for words, no more need for anything except rough movements followed by gentle ones, incoherent sounds of pleasure and the passionate struggle to share the core of joy that bonded them. They crested in a glorious moment when she begged Rucker to hold her tighter than ever, and he did. He gasped something so torn with passion and release that it wasn't until a few seconds later, as they lay trembling quietly in each other's arms, that she realized what it was.

My glorious possum queen. After she considered that strange compliment for a moment, she hugged him very hard and smiled tearfully against his shoulder.

•   •   •

The September morning was cold, barely touched by sunlight yet. Dinah huddled under her coverlet and blankets, feeling deliciously warm, in contrast. Something that smelled burnt and felt coarse brushed the soft underside of her nose. She wrinkled her upper lip, squinted, and pushed it away. It was replaced by something soft and tickling. She tried to brush that away, too, but it kissed her.

Her eyes opened wide. "Hmmmm," Rucker crooned against her mouth. "Good mornin'."

A sweet sense of anticipation melted through her as she looked up at him. He wasn't under the covers, he was kneeling beside her on the bed wearing only his jeans. "You have a nice morning face," she whispered. Dinah studied his half-closed eyes, the ruddy skin still flushed with sleep, the tossled hair, and slight beard shadow. "Very rumpled and sexy."

He chuckled. "Only problem is, I look like this 'til about noon." He kissed her again, this time longer. Then he brushed her tangled brunette hair back from her forehead and stroked her cheek. "Sleeping beauty," he murmured, his eyes roaming over her features. Dinah reveled in the pure adoration. She'd won dozens of titles, but she'd never felt so beautiful as now.

"Look," he said. He held up a piece of blackened bread. "I said the other day that I'd make you burnt toast for breakfast."

She laughed softly. "Thank you."

"I'm jokin'. I made a good breakfast. Sit up." He kissed her one more time and then began arranging pillows behind her. Dinah pulled herself upright and he carefully placed a plate on her lap. It was heaped with scrambled eggs and half a dozen pieces of nicely browned, not burnt, toast slathered with assorted jams. Rucker scooped raspberry on his fingertip, then dotted both her nipples with it. "Hmmm. Look at all the little goosebumps around the two big ones," he murmured. "I love cool weather." He leaned forward and cleaned the jam away with his tongue.

Dinah shifted as a white-hot rush of desire warmed her inside and out. The intensity of it surprised her.

After all, the night had been long and vigorous. Much like Rucker, she thought with rakish appreciation. She giggled.

"Now, that's a cute little sound for Madam Mayor to make," he teased. "I'd like to hear more of it."

Dinah covered her mouth, sincerely dismayed at the silly sound that had bubbled from it. "I'm not much of a giggler."

"All girls giggle. It's in their hormones."

"Be quiet, sexist oaf." They grinned at each other. He sat down beside her as she stared at the huge mound of food. "I hope we're going to share this," she noted.

"Yep." He retrieved a fork off her night stand, looking around as he did. "It's like one of those German furniture shops in here," he commented. "All contemporary."

"Scandinavian," she corrected drolly. "You mean Scandinavian."

He shrugged happily. They shared the fork, and he managed to drop food on her breasts with suspicious regularity so that he had to nibble and lick it off. By the time they finished she was practically sitting in his lap, and his jeans were undone. As her fingers tantalized him he groaned with pleasure.

"Where are our little friends?" he whispered into her ear.

Dinah smiled breathlessly at him. "All we have left are the purple ones."

He sighed with grand resignation. "The humiliation I go through to take you to ecstasy!"

After ecstasy—and it was ecstasy, she admitted when they lay blissfully quiet—they fell asleep again. When Dinah woke the next time he was propped up in bed, writing fervently on a big yellow pad balanced on his updrawn knees. The covers were tucked low around his waist, and he presented a very heart stopping masculine sight. But foreboding stirred inside her and chased away her sensual thoughts. Dinah lay very still and studied him, her brow furrowing in a quizzical frown.

"Doing a critique of me?" she asked with forced lightness.

He glanced over at her briefly and smiled. "You inspire me to write. Ssssh." He returned to his work. Dinah frowned harder. This was a new side of Rucker. He'd traded his lolling, carefree drawl for the crisp voice of business. His intense aura of concentration belied his image as a laid-back man. Obviously, he had a very serious, professional attitude where his writing was concerned. Always the journalist, she thought fearfully. Always the storyteller. And I'm a story. I let myself forget that.

She raised up on one elbow, feeling tension erase the shadows of sleep. "Are you really writing about me?" she persisted.

"Uh-huh. Good stuff, don't worry. Ssssh."

"For publication?"

"Well, not the stuff about your tattoos," he teased. "And not about us," he hurried to add. "That'd be too personal. Just about you. The way you run your town, and your life up here in Mount Pleasant. I'm gonna do a whole chapter about you and the town. I've been thinkin' about it the past few days. Now I'm sure."

"A whole chapter?" she repeated, her voice airy with fear. He didn't notice.

"Oh, yeah," he answered cheerfully. "For my next book. *Southern-Fried Gospel.* It's already under contract." He reached over and ruffled her dark hair with an affectionate gesture. "Let me work for a while, baby doll. Go back to sleep. Cute thing, you. Ssssh. This is important."

Baby doll. She stared at him with increasing anxiety and now a little annoyance. She was being dismissed like some fluffy playmate. "I think I'll take a bath," she muttered.

He kept writing. "Uh-huh," he said vaguely. "Feed my possum, please."

Dinah stayed in the bath tub a long time, thinking of ways to dissuade him from his determination to make her a celebrity. He absolutely could not write about her. What if Todd Norins saw the book and became curious enough to follow up on his old suspicions?

Dinah dressed in a creamy white jogging suit, plaited

her hair in a braid, put on light eye makeup, and padded barefoot out of the bathroom, her heart racing. Rucker was dressed in his jeans and Peevy-torn sweat-shirt from last night. He lay on his stomach amid the bed covers, writing so fast that she wondered how he'd be able to read the results. She sat on the foot of the bed and cleared her throat.

"Hmmm?" He glanced up, took her appearance in with an appreciative once-over, and whistled. "Vanilla ice cream. Nice. I'll be through with this in a minute." Then he returned to his work.

"Rucker? I know you won't understand why a politician wouldn't want publicity, and I know you're trying to compliment me, but . . . I really don't want to be a subject in your book. Or your column."

His head came up slowly, his green eyes surprised. He studied her so intensely that she looked away and fumbled with a loose thread on the side of her jogging pants. "Why not?" he asked.

"Well . . . I'm a very private person."

"Who used to parade around in tight bathing suits in order to win prizes," he noted drolly, smiling. "Come on, Dee, don't joke with me."

"I'm not joking." She paused, thinking over everything he'd just said. "And I know beauty pageants are partially just an excuse for showing off women's bod-ies, but there's a lot more to them than that. Don't make fun."

His smile faded. He sat up slowly and turned his pad facedown. Dinah's eyes widened in alarm as she noted that secretive action. "Something you don't want me to see?" she asked coolly.

"What's makin' you snap at dumb little things, Dee? You act like you think I'm plannin' to hurt you."

"Can I see what you've written there?" She nodded toward the pad.

His mouth, that wide, sensual mouth that could smile so easily, now tightened in determination. "No. It's a rough draft. There aren't many things I'm stubborn about, Dee, but my writing is one of them. It has to be perfect before I let anybody see it. Besides, I'm not gonna cater to your suspicions."

"So writing's a part of your life that you won't share with me?"

"I don't share rough drafts with anybody." He grasped her hand, and his expression softened. "Dee, you can trust me. Relax."

She held his hand desperately and looked deep into his eyes. "I want to, I really do." She took a steadying breath. "Rucker, I won't ask you for many favors, but I'm going to have to ask for this one. Don't write about me. Give me those notes or throw them away. Please."

"That's like askin' me to cut out part of my heart, Dee." He sat up and pulled her into his arms. Dinah looked at him with a silent, bittersweet plea, but he offered no mercy. "What is it, Dee?" he asked in a low, unyielding voice. He didn't sound angry, but he did sound exasperated and set on getting answers. "I think it's time you tell me what you're hidin' from."

"I simply don't like publicity."

"Lula Belle said you want to run for state senate some day. How are you gonna avoid the spotlight then?"

"Oh, that's just a—something I joke about."

"The hell it is. People told me you've already been approached by folks who'd help run your campaign."

Dinah exhaled hotly. "Running for state senate in Alabama wouldn't garner me national attention the way your books and columns would! And what have you been doing? Investigating me? Cajoling my friends for information?"

The subtle stiffening of his body told her that she'd hit a very big nerve. His eyes narrowed and he looked at her in grim disbelief. "You think that's why I asked them about you?"

She hesitated, telling herself that the man who'd made love to her so beautifully last night and this morning couldn't possibly be anyone to fear. *Tell him,* a firm inner voice goaded. *Tell him about the scandal that ruined your father's life, the scandal that was indirectly responsible for his death. The scandal that nearly ruined your life, and still might.*

Dinah fought the band of steel that enveloped her throat, but she'd lived with secrecy so long, she'd protected herself so carefully for so many years, that the words couldn't escape. "I want to trust you," she whispered in an anguished voice.

"But you don't." His deep voice was full of pain, anger, and bewilderment. "I can't believe it! After what we shared last night. After the things we did together, there's still a part of you that thinks I'm nothing but a fast talkin' con artist lookin' for a story."

"No! Oh, Rucker . . ." Her eyes filled with tears. She pushed herself away and moved to the end of the bed, turning her back to him. "I just—it's just a matter of dignity. What you write is funny and insightful. It's terrific entertainment. But I don't want to be anyone's entertainment. I don't want to be talked about or laughed about by strangers."

His voice was deadly. "Dee, tell me the damned truth. I smell lies like a dog smells a trail and I won't put up with them. You tell me what's wrong, and you tell me right now, little lady."

Little lady. She whipped around, her chin thrust forward. "You won't put up with them?" she echoed curtly. "You'll tell me what to do, and I'd better do it, is that it?"

"That's right! There can only be one top dog in this argument, and you're lookin' straight at him."

"Indeed! I think you mean that you expect me to be a docile little bed bunny who'll let you boss her around!"

"I expect you not to keep secrets from me and accuse me of stupid things!"

"I expect you not to turn my town and my private life into a circus of corny jokes for a national audience to snicker over!"

That was the final blow. He stood and methodically ripped his work out of the big note pad. He folded the sheets with fierce, sharp movements of his fingers then stuck the parcel in his back pocket. Dinah stood also, her heart catching. What now? "Please tear those notes up," she begged. "That's all I ask. Is it so much, if you really care about me?"

His hands clenched by his sides. "If you really care about me, you'll say why you don't trust me."

"I do . . . want to trust you." She held out her hands in supplication. "Rucker, I've been through a lot, things that I *will* tell you about, if you'll be patient."

"Seems to me, if you ask a man into your bed, and you say that he's special, and you do things with him that you say you've never done with anyone else, that you ought to trust him already."

Dinah knew then that the situation was hopeless. "You don't see shades of gray, do you," she said wearily. "That's one reason people enjoy your writing so much. You see things the way they ought to be, and you never yield an inch." She laughed bitterly. "That's very commendable."

"You don't yield much, either, Dee. You've got all sorts of things hidden inside you, and you've got a wall of pride ten feet thick around you."

They shared a long, tortured look. She refused to let herself cry, but the effort from not crying made it difficult to talk. He seemed to be having difficulty with his own emotions. "Everything's happened so fast," she finally managed. "You showed up here . . . just five days ago . . ."

"Doesn't matter," he said gruffly. "You know that's not the problem. Five days. People fall in love in five days. Five hours, sometimes. Five minutes."

"Some people do," she answered hoarsely. Now was not the time to acknowledge that they were in love with each other. It would only add misery to misery. "Some people only get caught up in physical temptation."

She felt sick when she saw how harshly her insinuation affected him. For a moment he seemed incapable of speaking. Then he ground words out through clenched teeth. "Some people know how to stab right to the heart."

"Rucker," she cried, unable to bear the pain she'd caused him. "Rucker—"

But he had already turned and was walking out the bedroom door. Dinah followed him silently, knowing that this was the end of the beginning, their beginning. They hadn't even had a chance to make things work. He went down the hall to the living room, removed his jacket from a sleek brass coat stand by the front door, then walked over to a chaise lounge covered in white damask. The possum was curled there, asleep. He scooped it up gently and placed it in the crook of one arm. Then he went to the front door and pulled it open.

He turned, assessed her with cold eyes, and said simply, "I reckon you know how to find me in Birmingham, if it matters."

She nodded. "It matters," she answered brokenly.

His jaw worked for a second, but he either couldn't or didn't want to say anything else. He went through the door, slammed it behind him, and walked across the porch without looking back.

Dinah felt as if she were strangling on sorrow. Turning, she fled to the sunny sanctuary of her kitchen, sat down at the table, and put her face in her hands, where she kept it as she listened to the Cadillac leave. Then the morning was silent, achingly silent except for the small sounds Nureyev made as he ruffled his feathers. He cackled something incoherently. He tried again, with better results. Dinah raised her head and stared at him.

"Dee!" he squawked. "Hot . . . damn!"

For a second, she was so startled that she wanted to laugh. Rucker had left his outrageous imprint on her life in every way that he could, even to coaching her intellectual crow in good-old-boy lingo. Now he's gone, Dinah told herself. And it's for the best. Tears slipped quietly down her face.

Six

"Boss, if you want pictures of beautiful, leggy women, why don't you go back to your office and look through your collection of *Sports Illustrated* swimsuit issues?" Millie's annoyed voice echoed through the newspaper's research room as she plunked down a new box of microfilm from the file drawers.

Rucker huffed a vague sound of dismissal at her and kept studying the murky screen before him. "I'm lookin' for articles, not pictures, articles about one leggy woman in particular. Get me the . . . hmmm . . . yeah, check our Sunday magazines from about seven years ago. Must have had some sort of fluffy profile on the current Miss Georgia." Her short, athletic body full of purpose, Millie glided away.

"Here's one!" she exclaimed a few minutes later. "Beethoven, Beauty, and Brains: Georgia's Triple-Threat Beauty Queen Has What It Takes To Be Top Contender For Miss America." Rucker leaped up and took the microfilm card she held out, then quickly placed it in the viewer. Millie bent over his shoulder as he scanned through the pages of the old magazine section. "Shoo!" she commented sardonically. "Broiler hens, twenty-nine cents a pound. And to think I was in the Navy then, and missed that buy."

"Hush up, you tart-tongued little amazon," Rucker ordered. She laughed. He found the page he wanted and studied it fervently. It contained a photograph of a younger, slightly thinner Dinah, with short, carefully styled hair. She was in full Miss Georgia regalia: tiara, roses, sash, antebellum gown, bright smile, and gleaming eyes. He forgot that Millie was beside him and gently placed the tip of one forefinger to the photograph as if he were touching Dinah's face. I love you, he admitted silently. I'm going crazy to see you again.

From the corner of his eye, he caught Millie shifting in embarrassment and he realized that his expression revealed everything. Rucker jerked his hand away from the photograph. "Ever seen a woman with that many pearly teeth before in your life?" he drawled nonchalantly. "Not too bad lookin' for one of those debutante types, is she? She looks even better now. Got a little more meat on her."

His ruse didn't work. Millie patted his shoulder sympathetically. "She's beautiful, Rucker," she said gently. "You have good taste." She paused. "I hope that some day a man looks at me the way you just looked at her."

"Somebody will, gorgeous." He paused. "Thanks, Millie, for carin'." Rucker sighed. When tough little Millie started treating him with kindness, he knew that his misery had become embarrassingly obvious. He grumbled abruptly, "Why don't you go find a mailroom boy to kung fu, Miss Hunstomper?"

She patted his shoulder again and left the research room. Rucker read the article hurriedly, frowning. Damn! Basics, that's all this was. "I believe in the American political system," Dinah told the reporter. "I'd like to use my abilities in a leadership role to solve the crises of poverty, war, and hatred in the world." His brows arched at that quote.

There was no poverty in Mount Pleasant, very little hatred, and the only war had been a nasty skirmish one year between the Baptist Women's League and the Methodist Women's League over which group was going to host the Shriners' Appreciation Luncheon. He looked at Dinah's old photograph in sad bewilderment. What had become of the idealistic young woman who appeared so ready to tackle the world's problems?

He read on. She said that her father, Bill Sheridan,

was her guiding force and biggest supporter. President of First Georgia Trust, one of the state's largest banks. She'd said he was the most honorable man she knew. Rucker hurt for her, knowing that her father had died in the plane crash only a few months after this article was published. He glanced at the credits. Story by Todd Norins. Special to the *Herald Examiner*. Todd Norins. That was a familiar name.

He called Millie on a phone in the research room. "Know who Todd Norins is?" he asked.

"Rucker! Who doesn't?"

"I doesn't," he protested.

"He's the top investigative reporter on *USA Personal*. It's like *60 Minutes*, only without class. A big hit. Sleazy, muckraking, network TV show. Ugh." She paused, then added in a guilty voice, "I watch it every week."

"I'm comin' back to my office. Get me a phone number for Mr. Muck."

A few minutes later, seated amid his comfortable clutter, his boots propped on top of a scarred, much-abused computer terminal, Rucker listened to the telephone ring at a New York connection. He cajoled a receptionist until he convinced her that yes, he was the same Rucker McClure who'd written her favorite book, *Down Home Swamp Stories*. She put him through to one secretary, who put him through to the *USA Personal* secretary, who hemmed and hawed but finally said she'd see if Mr. Norins was available.

"Norins here," a booming voice said eventually. "What can I do for the redneck king of corny schmaltz?"

. Rucker absorbed the greeting thoughtfully. It was one thing for one southerner to call another a redneck, but something else for an outside to use the term. "Howdy, Norins. Heard that you're the terror of boob tube journalism. Sort of top boob."

Rucker listened to a snorting laugh on the New York side of the line. Hell, the guy sounds like Ted Baxter on *The Mary Tyler Moore Show*, he thought.

"Good shot. What can I do for you, McClure?"

"Been researching a gal you once interviewed. Recall a Dinah Sheridan, Miss Georgia from about six years ago? Walked out on the Miss America pageant after her father bought the farm in a Cessna crash?"

"Certainly. I was covering the pageant for *Amazing World* back then, before I hit the big time."

"Oh. The big time bein' television, instead of print journalism?"

"Well, you know what I mean. I hated to leave my job at *Amazing World*, but I had the kind of talent that the TV news execs were willing to pay big bucks for."

"Must have been hell, givin' up *Amazing World*," Rucker answered slyly. "Helluva lot of prestige. I read it every week." He added silently, In the grocery store check-out line. Then I put it right back on the rack next to the antacid mints and cheap candy. How appropriate.

"Yes, thank you. Well, at any rate, McClure, what's the scoop on Dinah Sheridan? Wonderful girl. We were great pals." Rucker thought there was something calculated about Norin's sincerity, but he reminded himself that all TV people sounded that way. "What's become of her?" Norins persisted.

Rucker shrugged. He couldn't see any reason not to chat openly with the guy. "Well, she's mayor of Mount Pleasant, Alabama. Great little one-drink, Bible Belt place right out of a Norman Rockwell painting. Teaches history at the local high school, coaches the drill team, organizes a funky little festival called 'Possum Days'. . ."

"Mount Pleasant, Alabama. Bible Belt," Norins intoned slowly, as if he were making notes. "Teacher. Mayor. Coach. Sounds like Miss American Pie. Very respectable. Got it."

"I went up there to absorb some backwoods color, and I got curious about her. That incident with the Miss America pageant. You were real close to that. Did you know something that never hit the papers? About why she walked out, I mean?"

There was a long, careful pause. "Oh, it was just grief over her old man's death. You understand how chicks are."

"Not lately," Rucker muttered under his breath.

"So tell me more about her. Well-built chick, even if she was too brainy and intimidating. Not very feminine in those ways."

Rucker frowned at that condescending description of Dinah and silently mouthed several choice obscenities at the phone. He suspected that any woman with an IQ higher than a turnip's was too brainy and intimidating for Norins. Rucker's instinctive wariness of the man blossomed into pure dislike, and after making small talk for another minute, he thanked him for his time and said a terse good-bye.

Afterwards Rucker sat unmoving, staring blankly at the stack of books he kept by his phone. They were for the times when his creative muses felt like taking a break, which had been often in the days since he left Mount Pleasant. Pat Conroy, Joyce Carol Oates, Ernest Hemingway—Rucker looked at the authors' names without seeing them. Millie finally stuck her head in the door. "Are you all right?" she asked.

He looked up at her, feeling worried for reasons he couldn't quite fathom. "Did you ever watch *The Mary Tyler Moore Show*?"

"Devotedly."

"Would you say that Ted Baxter was a good guy or a bad guy?"

"What?" She arched one blond brow. "Did somebody hit you in the head with a golf ball recently?"

"Aw, never mind." He waved her away and propped his chin on one hand. Todd Norins is okay, he assured himself. A jerk, but harmless. Now what? Rucker had been digging for a week, and he still had no clue to Dinah's mysterious fears. There was only one thing left to do. Take the offensive. Rucker turned to his terminal and clicked the power on.

Dinah walked out of her classroom at the end of fifth-period Constitutional Studies and was met by Myra Faye, whose corpulent face had flushed a hue that matched her frilly rose blouse. Myra Faye held out the afternoon edition of the *Birmingham Herald/Examiner*, the newspaper that served Mount Pleasant. "Rucker wrote about us again!" she told Dinah excitedly. "It's been two weeks since he was here, and I figured he decided not to write any more about us. But look!"

Her heart pounding with dread, Dinah took the folded section of the paper and hurriedly studied the column, which was headlined "Possums and the Good Life." Other teachers gathered around, peering over her shoulders. Dinah finished reading and mused slowly, "He didn't mention my name."

"Well . . . I'm sure he meant to," Myra Faye offered awkwardly.

Dinah looked up and saw the sympathy on her round face. "Oh, no, Myra Faye," she explained quickly, "I'm not upset." Around her, she saw people smiling over what Rucker had written.

"He made Wally Oscar sound almost normal," one of the other teachers commented.

"And the football team hasn't had such a good write-up since they beat Mount Clarion seventy-two to three, in a hail storm," someone else said. "And that was eight years ago."

Dinah looked back at the article. "It's wonderful," she admitted in a small voice. "I'll have a copy framed and put it up in my office at city hall." Oh, Rucker, is this an invitation to forgive and forget? I hope so, she added silently. A half-dozen times she'd started to phone him during the past two weeks but stopped in each instance, knowing that he wanted to hear more than her sorrowful "I miss you. I didn't mean to hurt you." He wanted the truth behind her fears, and she still wasn't ready to reveal it.

"You gotta call him and say thanks," Myra Faye urged.

"I suppose you're right. It's the polite thing to do."

"If you're goin' to Birmingham for that conference next Monday, why don't you stop by and thank him in person? I'll send him a cream-cheese pound cake."

"I'll send some muscadine preserves!" noted Alice Dallyroo, head of the home economics department.

"I'll have my seniors make a thank-you card," chimed Glen Norton, the art teacher.

Dinah looked around her in dismay. She was the only person in Mount Pleasant who was trying to resist Rucker's appeal, and even she wasn't doing very well at it, because now that she had an excuse to visit him, she found herself wanting to whoop like a cheerleader.

The newsroom of *The Birmingham Herald/Examiner* was huge, and Dinah felt very self-conscious as she trudged across it under the appreciative stares of nearly a dozen male reporters. Her hands felt sweaty on the big cardboard box that held presents for Rucker. Her knees trembled under the slender skirt of her blue-gray suit, and the heels of her gray pumps seemed to thud loudly even on the carpeted floor.

As Dinah neared the far side of the room, a pretty, petite blonde looked up from a desk in a cluttered cubicle next to a closed door. Dinah felt her pulse accelerate as she noted the boldly hand-lettered sign—Rucker's handwriting, Dinah deduced—taped to the cubicle's outer wall. Beware of Miss Hunstomper, it read. She Bites. I'm in the right place, Dinah acknowledged. Rucker's office is behind the closed door.

The blond dynamo, dressed in a flowing green dress, leaped up and came out of the cubicle almost at a run. "I'm Millie," she beamed. "I was relieved to get your phone call, Mayor Sheridan. The boss has been a mess."

Me, too, Dinah told her silently. "Call me Dinah." She smiled politely at Millie, but her eyes shifted to the closed door. "Did you tell Rucker that I'd be stopping by?"

"No, he hasn't come back from lunch yet." Millie led the way to Rucker's office, opened the door, and swept one hand out in a grand gesture. "Make yourself at home. I have to run some errands for one of the editors."

Dinah stepped inside, looking at the tiny room in amazement. There wasn't a spare inch of unused space. "Are there walls under all these . . . decorations?"

Millie made a huffing sound. "I'm afraid to take anything down and look."

She left the door open and trotted off on business. Dinah heard a male reporter calling coyly to her and

Millie's growling, "Stow it, sucker." Miss Hunstomper was strange but likable, similar to everything and everyone else Rucker brought into his life. Like me? Dinah considered wryly.

She set her box and purse down on a stack of newspapers that occupied the office's only guest chair. Then she sidled between the desk and a huge hanging plant, intending to study the walls a little closer. But the plant, which had vines as long as ten feet, caught on her arm. She looked at it closely and couldn't keep from chuckling.

"Kudzu! I should have known. He has a weed for an office plant!"

She turned her curious gaze back to the walls, and her eyes widened in awe. There, scattered among sports calendars, posters, tractor caps, tennis rackets, a broken, bronzed golf club, and a plaque naming Rucker an honorary Boy Scout, were the chronicles of an impressive career. She studied his writing awards, his photographs with celebrities he'd interviewed, his reviews, both good and bad—only a secure, mellow man displays bad reviews, she thought, with a sense of respect—and the framed covers of his books.

She saw at least a dozen photographs that could only be Rucker's family: the tall, plump mother tearfully hugging a full-length fur coat that must have been a gift from him; the dead truck-driver father, raw-boned and stern; a handsome, stalwart sister who shared Rucker's auburn hair and mischievous eyes. Dinah tapped the sister's photograph and told her, "You're a rascal, I'd bet."

"She used to knock the stuffin' out of me."

Dinah whirled around, her mouth open in surprise. Rucker stood in the doorway, looking as shocked as she felt. Her heart in her throat, Dinah noted vaguely that his height nearly filled the door frame, that his eyes were just as soulful as she remembered, that he was the kind of rugged looking man who drew a woman's rapt attention whenever he entered a room. Especially now, in this exceedingly small room, which gave her only a tiny bit of safety space. The sight of him brought back every memory of their tempestuous night together.

"Hi," she murmured.

"Howdy."

He wore a nondescript tweed sport coat, a white shirt, no tie, jeans, and his black boots. Virility in a casual but effective package, she thought nervously. He shut the door, closing the two of them off from the rest of the world. His gaze moved slowly over her, then back to her eyes.

"What can I do for you?" he asked gruffly.

Excitement and uncertainty hovered in the air between them. Dinah clasped her hands in front of her to hide their shaking. She nodded to the cardboard box, and eventually he removed his gaze from her and glanced at it. "Everyone loved your article. They sent gifts. Everything's labeled, so you'll know who to thank." She cleared her throat. "There's also . . . a copy of an official letter from myself to your newspaper's publisher. I thought I should write him and say how much the article meant to . . . to everyone in Mount Pleasant."

"Thanks."

"Yes. Well. How are you?"

"Fine."

Dinah trained her eyes on his golf bag, which was propped by the corner of his desk. The leather had his initials sewn on it in gold letters, she noted. RAM. She wondered vaguely what the A stood for. Aggressive? Aggravating? Since he seemed intent on forcing her to grovel, he was certainly both of those.

"I'm in town for a regional conference of mayors," she explained. "I thought I'd just stop by."

"Just stop by, huh?" he mimicked, taking a step toward her. She looked up warily, her lips parted, her face burning. "Guess you expect me to take you to dinner tonight, or somethin'."

Dinah squinted at him defensively. "You egomaniac." She hadn't figured on this taunting from him. He was so stern.

"Oh, I want to take you to dinner. We're gonna talk."

"The conference won't end until seven."

"I'll wait."

"It's at the Sheraton."

"I'll be in the main lobby."

Dinah smoothed her skirt and straightened her shoulders. "I have to go now," she reported coolly. "Back to the bed—I mean, back to the conference." Dinah bit her tongue and looked at him solemnly from under her brows. He returned the expression perfectly. She wanted to wrap the Kudzu plant around herself and hide in shame. *Bed? What was wrong with her mind?*

"Did I say anything about bed?" he asked innocently. "I'll walk you down to the elevator, Dee." He took her arm primly, scooped her purse up, and guided her out of the office.

At the elevator she turned and looked up at him with wary, searching eyes. "My slip about 'bed' wasn't meant to be Freudian innuendo," she warned.

He arched one brow. "Now who's an egomaniac? I don't intend to dive into 'physical temptation' again, so don't worry."

Her mouth thinned as she recalled the awful insinuation she'd made two weeks ago when she'd implied that their night together was based on lust rather than love. Dinah wanted to tell him that it had been no more than a stupid defensive maneuver. The elevator opened behind her, but she didn't notice until Rucker gently prodded her. She stepped into it and stood looking at him with a quizzical expression on her face. *Aren't you even going to try to seduce me tonight?* she felt like demanding. His neutrality frightened her. She'd kept saying that they weren't compatible, and now he seemed to believe it too.

"Seven o'clock," she said primly, her chin up.

"Uh-huh. And we'll go to my house." Dinah's aplomb deserted her and she stared at him with her mouth open. As the elevator doors closed he almost seemed to be smiling.

Neat. His house was neat. And exceptionally clean. And very well decorated in a pleasing mixture of sturdy country styles and early American antiques. Dinah couldn't get over her astonishment as they walked through the main floor. He waved a frosty mug of beer this way and that, describing how he tussled with the decorator over styles.

"And I told that lady," he said sternly, "I said, 'If you put a Chippendale chair over yonder in that spot, I'm likely to sit in it. And if I bust it, I'll feel real bad, because it cost a lot of money. Put the antiques out of my way, and put the real furniture where I can enjoy it. And don't bring any more paintin's of naked babies with wings!'"

"You mean cherubs?" Despite the strained mood, Dinah wanted to laugh so badly that she almost choked on a sip of wine. She took a firmer grip on her ornate crystal wine glass—another oddity in the unfolding vision of Rucker's home life. She'd assumed that his crystal consisted of a few Mason jars and cartoon glasses.

"Yeah, cherubs," he huffed. "Silly things."

They entered a cozy den that overlooked a huge deck, a pool, a Jacuzzi, and a beautifully manicured back yard dotted with big hardwoods. The den had a big stone fireplace with an overstuffed, dark blue couch in front of it.

"This is a wonderful home," she told him sincerely. "It has a good, masculine feel to it. It's comfortable. I like it a great deal."

"You haven't even seen the upstairs," he said proudly. "But that's not important." The front door bell chimed. "Well. Time to eat."

She made no comment and took another sip of wine. His bedroom was upstairs, and apparently he didn't want to get her anywhere near it. That's good, isn't it? she reminded herself grimly. "Dinner is being delivered?" she inquired. "Pizza? Girl Scout cookies?"

He laughed and pointed in the direction of an elegant dining room she'd visited earlier. "Go sit down and be impressed with my fancy china and clean table cloth. I'll take care of the food."

Dinner was provided by a gourmet catering service, as it turned out, and it was splendid. But she noted that Rucker made no attempt to create a romantic atmosphere. The overhead chandelier provided soft but bright light, and he kept up a stream of careful small talk that contained no innuendo. After dinner, they carried cups of coffee into the den. He built a fire while Dinah watched from the couch.

"It's really nippy outside tonight," she commented. "The fire is very cozy. This is good sleeping weather." Darkness had closed around the house, making the den intimate. Then Rucker switched on a brass lamp near the couch. Drat, Dinah told him silently. What does all this nonaggression mean?

He sat down a proper distance away from her, leaned forward, stared into the fire, and sipped his coffee. "So," he murmured, "we've gotta talk."

"Yes."

"That article about Mount Pleasant was bait, and you bit the hook. You comin' to see me today tells me that you've missed me. At least, you've missed me in bed."

Dinah gave him an angry, hurt look. "Maybe I've missed you for general reasons. Maybe I was sorry when you left. Maybe I ought to have my head examined for wanting to see a man who compares me to a fish."

"But we're not compatible," he said sarcastically.

"Oh." She frowned into her coffee cup. "Yes, that's what I said."

"Plus, I want to write about you and you don't want me to."

"Yes."

"Plus, you live in Mount Pleasant and I live two hours away, in Birmingham. Makes it hard to see each other."

"I hadn't even thought of that," she noted dully.

"But the worst thing is, you don't trust me. And I can't bear that, Dee." The words were spoken simply, without rebuke. "A man and a woman—if they don't have trust, they don't have anything. My parents had problems, and lack of trust was one of 'em. My ex-wife . . ." His voice trailed off. "Well, trust is real important to me."

Dinah winced. She looked up and found him studying her, his eyes hooded. Feeling hopeless and distraught, she got up and walked to the fireplace, where she stood with her back turned to him. "I wish you could give me time," she said in a voice laced with anguish. "I wish you could understand and find a way to be patient." She smacked the mantel with one hand and spoke in a voice that threatened to shatter. "Damn it! You're the stubbornest man I've ever known!"

"Good! Good! I don't want to be like the simperin', smarmy-butt men you've dated all your life!" he retorted.

"Smarmy b-bu . . . what in the world?"

"You can't ice me over with those blue eyes and you can't buffalo me with your smarts! I say what I mean and mean what I say! And I'm gonna treat you like a normal woman, not like some princess!"

He vaulted up and strode to the fireplace, shoved his coffee cup onto the mantel, and faced her with his hands on his blue-jeaned hips. He'd traded his sport coat and shirt for a green, holey pullover sweater. It clung snugly to his chest as he inhaled in anger.

Dinah jabbed a finger at him. "You want everything your own way! You won't relent! You won't give me any privacy—"

"I will, damn it, if you'll quit talkin' long enough to listen!"

"Me? Who yabbers nonstop in this duo. You will what? What will you do? Drive me crazy?"

He grabbed her shoulders roughly. "I *will* let you keep your secrets!" he yelled. "I won't write about you! What else do you want me to say?"

"I . . . I don't know," she stammered.

"I can have patience, Dee," he thundered, "if you can do one thing for *me!*"

"What?" she whispered.

"Tell me the truth about what you said two weeks ago! About that 'physical temptation' stuff bein' all that we had goin'! Did you really mean that I'm only important to you in bed?"

"Oh, Rucker." She reached up and grabbed his hands in hers. "I never thought that. I never meant to hurt you the way I did."

He took a viselike grip of her hands and shook them. "Do you love me? Will you admit that what's goin' on between us can already be called love?"

"All right!" she exclaimed in exasperation. "It is! I've never felt anything like it before! It's unique! Wonderful! Terrifying! I love you, you big oaf! I love—"

He jerked her into his arms and kissed her roughly. Dinah murmured in surprise and then delight. She flung her arms around his neck and kissed him back as hard as she could. He slid his lips off hers for a second and said, "We got it, Dee. We got the best thing goin' in the whole world. I don't ever want to hear you say that damned word again. *Compatible*." He made a grandly derisive sound. "Not ever! Not once!"

"Done, sir!" She stroked his back with long, desperate movements of her hands, her head tilted back and her eyes half closed. "Do you really mean it? You won't write anything?"

"Little lady, I give you my word. And when I give my word—"

"I understand. Oh, Rucker." Her voice dropped. "Some day I'll try to explain why I feel so defensive."

"You're damned right you will." She looked at him with warning and his voice softened to a comically submissive level. "Uh, whenever you want to."

"Big, macho, bossy," she said with a ragged, affectionate tone, "chauvinistic, domineering—"

He captured the last words before they fully left her lips, sweeping his mouth across hers. He pushed and she pulled and they sank to the plushly carpeted floor as if on some silent cue, undoing each other's clothes, murmuring soft, sweet words that gentled the impatient physical and emotional forces between them. When they lay naked in each other's arms, the carpet formed a delicious dark cushion under Dinah's bare skin. She felt as if she were glowing with firelight and passion as Rucker braced himself over her. She looked into his eyes and their reckless desire absorbed her. Her hands stroked his chest roughly.

"You be still," he ordered, and guided her hands to the carpet.

"I will not," she protested lightly.

"You will too. I have ways, ways of makin' you be still."

He trailed his mouth across her breasts and down to her stomach, where he tormented the silky skin with damp, greedy kisses. Dinah felt her body becoming deliciously heavy, as if it were sinking deeper and deeper into the carpet. She moaned, and Rucker chuckled in a hoarse way that was both smugly victorious and vulnerable. He quickly slid further downward and parted her thighs.

"I have ways," he repeated in a languid whisper, and then he was too preoccupied to talk.

"Oh, yes," she managed, her head thrown back and her hands tangled in his hair. There was no way to be modest or reserved with Rucker, and for the first time in her life she felt free to react any way she wanted. He drew sensation through her until she begged him without embarrassment not to stop. She knew that he watched her, and she reveled in his encouragement. She dug her heels into the deep carpet and let reality disappear as happiness flowed out of her in second after second of shattering pleasure.

He scooped her into his arms afterwards and carried her upstairs to his room, where she laughed gently over the rumpled bed and general disarray. This was the real Rucker. "I'll show you how to mess up the bed even more," he promised in a gruff voice. And he did, gloriously, so that one by one the pillows tumbled onto the floor and the satiny black bedspread soon followed. Afterwards he lay sprawled in happy exhaustion on his back in the middle of all the ruin, smiling. Dinah snuggled close by his side, held in the possessive embrace of his arm, nuzzling his neck.

"I know this is love, Dee," he sighed. "Because I'll do anything to make you happy. I'll—why, hell, I'll even read that Satire boy you're so fond of."

She thought for a moment. "Sartre," she corrected wryly. "Sartre."

"Yeah." He twisted his head and kissed her nose so that his mustache tickled it. "That's him."

Dinah traced his collarbones with her fingertip. "I'll . . . I'll learn to like country-western music," she told him sincerely. "And . . . golf! You can teach me how to play golf!"

He sighed again, a long, contented reaction that seemed to start at his head and end at his toes. It captured Dinah, and she sighed too. For tonight, at least, the world is perfect, she admitted. And she decided not to worry about anything else.

Seven

"More shortening, Dee! Dad burnit, woman, fried chicken is supposed to be greasy! Aaah! What are you doing! Stop that!"

"It's just paprika and oregano!"

"No, hon, no! This isn't Italian chicken, it's Dixie chicken! The only thing you put on it is salt and pepper!" Rucker grabbed the herb jars from her and put them back in her kitchen cabinet, then sighed with grand relief. He dumped a large white chunk of lard into the already greasy skillet and nodded happily.

Dinah stomped one foot in amused protest. "Do you want your arteries to look like the inside of a deep fat fryer?"

"My grandpa Elmo ate fried chicken almost every day of his life, and he lived to be a hundred!"

"Ouch!" Dinah jerked her hand away as grease splattered from the huge skillet. She looked at Rucker indignantly as she rubbed a burn on her wrist. "I want combat pay," she said.

He wiped his hands on the towel tucked in the band of his gray jogging sweats. "Ooooh, poor darlin'," he crooned, taking her wrist in one big hand. He raised it to his mouth and licked the injured area with small, gentle movements of his tongue, while his green eyes crinkled at her in laughter. Then he pressed her wrist to his breast, which was covered in a white sweatshirt

bearing the logo "Not tonight, dear. I have a deadline."
"Does it feel better now?" he purred. "Poor sweetie."

"Oh, don't patronize me." Smiling jauntily, she pulled
her hand away from him and looked at the skillet
crammed with floured chicken pieces. They crackled
and sizzled and, she admitted, gave off a wonderful
scent. Outside the kitchen window, the October wind
made cold whooshing sounds under the eaves, and the
night was an impenetrable black shield beneath a rainy
sky. But inside, the lights were cheerful and the kitchen
warm. The caress of her silky, white nightgown added
even more to her sense of being deliciously pampered.

Rucker had brought the gown to her this weekend in
a big, gift-wrapped box from one of the city's most
exclusive women's lingerie shops. The box also contained garter belts, teddies, and a half-dozen other
gorgeous, glamorous, sexy things. They were, he said
solemnly, an anniversary present in honor of their first
month together. Amazing, she'd thought with tears of
pleasure gleaming in her eyes. They're beautiful. He
doesn't know how to pick out a pair of matching socks
for himself, but he's magnificent at selecting things for
me to wear. Whenever she pictured Rucker invading a
lingerie shop on her behalf, her eyes grew misty with
tender amusement.

Of course, Dinah thought wryly as she touched the
delicate lace of her bodice, I'll never get a chance to
wear this gown or any other to bed with him. He was,
in his own words, "a believer in bare bohunkus sleepin'."
She hadn't the nerve to ask what a *bohunkus* was.

Nureyev walked back and forth on his perch, always
alert for a handout. The possum was crunching dry cat
food from a bowl in the floor. Rucker finished turning
chicken pieces over with a fork and gestured toward
his squat gray pet. "I forgot to tell you, Dee! I named
my baby!"

"Oh? 'Rucker, Junior'?"

He waved the fork with mock menace. "Hah. Something cultured. Like Nureyev is named after that male
ballet dancer." He paused, nodding for emphasis. "Well,
I named the possum Jethro."

"Jethro? What cultural figure is that?"

"Jethro Bodine, from *The Beverly Hillbillies*. My idol." He dodged the scrap of biscuit dough she flung at him in a pretense of disgust. "Check the oven," he commanded. "My cupcakes should nearly be done."

Smiling, Dinah bent over her white electric stove and cracked the door open. Two dozen chocolate cupcakes were baking inside. Chocolate cupcakes with raisins and little multi-colored sprinkles embedded in the chocolate. She grimaced. Rucker's beloved dessert was suitable for a grammar school picnic but not much else.

"They look fine, relatively speaking." She slipped an oven mitt on her hand and retrieved the cupcake pans, then put them on the counter beside a bowl of mushy potato salad and a wicker basket of giant biscuits oozing butter.

"Rucker?" she crooned in an innocent voice. "As you get older are you planning to develop one of those stomachs that hangs over a belt? You know, the hard, pear-shaped kind that pushes your belt buckle down and makes you appear swaybacked?"

"You smart-mouthed ladybug!" In one quick movement he grabbed her and hoisted her over his shoulder.

"Rucker, stop it!" He was always trying to break down her dignified reserve, and she knew from experience that he wouldn't quit this time until he was successful. "This isn't funny!"

"Sure 'nuff *is* funny," he drawled. "I should know. I write funny stuff for a livin'."

Dinah hung upside down with her rump next to his head, and he ran devilish, tickling fingers under the hem of her clingy gown. "You makin' fun of my good country food," he demanded, "the way you made fun of me when I got bubble gum in my mustache last week?"

"The way you make fun of *me* for laying out my clothes at night!" She wiggled and shoved.

His fingers did a spider walk up the back of her thigh, and he chuckled fiendishly. "Panties on the left," he said in a high-pitched imitation of her voice. "Bra on the right. Slip in the middle." Chuckling harder, he let his voice drop to normal. "You *never* do it any different. I'm gonna rearrange everything and watch the next mornin' to see if you get bumfuddled and put your panties on your head." He turned his mouth toward her squirming hip, howled like a wolf, and bit the silk-covered curve gently.

"Rucker!" Struggling, convulsing with laughter, she tried to kick, but he clamped her long legs with one arm and let his fingers tickle the quivering, naked rump at the top of them.

"Giggle," he ordered. "Come on, Madam Mayor. You can do it. Any woman who thinks books about economics are light reading needs to learn to giggle!"

"I don't like to giggle!"

He began gnawing at her hip, taking the nightgown between his teeth and growling. Dinah pressed her hands over her mouth and fought the sounds that wanted to burst out. This scene was representative of the past four weeks with Rucker—giddy, joyful, lighthearted. They spent every spare day together, every spare moment, and talked for hours on the phone when he was out of town making a speech or at home in Birmingham. She had never been so happy before in her life.

"Guggle!" he demanded again, his voice muffled by a mouthful of silk. "Guggle!"

She giggled, her hands fell loosely down his back, and she pressed her face into his sweatshirt. "H-happy now, y-you idiot?"

"Uh-huh." His hand roamed over her rump with disarming intimacy. He spat out the fabric. "Got a little extra paddin' here," he observed in a rakish voice. " 'For you know it, you'll get those little dimples and then things'll start to sprrrread, and—"

"I'm very disciplined and I work out with weights! I'm not going to spread!"

"Aw, yes, Miss Discipline. Hmmm. Let's see. This muscle feels okay, I guess." His fingers dipped and explored with unfettered delight. "That one is tight. Ooooh, and that one is plumb athletic!"

"Put me down!" Giggling uncontrollably now, she pinched his flat, masculine hips lightly through his jogging pants. Yelping, he set her back on her feet. Her face flushed, she grasped his shoulders and looked up at him with a wobbly grin. "You adolescent fiend," she said.

His eyes glowed with devotion that she cherished. In the skillet the chicken made a robust, sizzling sound. Rucker glanced at it, then back at her. "Thank you for lettin' me teach you how to cook," he said sweetly.

"Mr. McClure, I *know* how to cook. This"—she waved her hand at the array of his favorite foods—"is not cooking. This is . . . this is a cholesterol nightmare!"

He looked a little crestfallen, and she hugged him. "But I love it," she lied.

"You're tellin' a big fat fib," he noted with exaggerated petulance.

"Never say 'big' or 'fat' to a woman who's about to eat her weight in fried chicken."

"I'll love you even if you spread a whole lot," he said, and hugged her back. "I love you, Dee. Love you. Hmmm, hmmm." He rocked her from side to side, his arms tightening. "What a gal. Had a four-point average in college. Always looks chick. That's *chic*, if you say it in French."

Dinah sighed contentedly inside the strong circle of his arms, but a nagging inner voice made her say, "I wish life would stay this pleasant."

She felt Rucker's lips on her dark hair. "You got a cynical streak, Dee. Don't look so hard for trouble."

"I'm sorry. I suppose I feel that everything happy comes to a tragic end."

His hand stroked her back as the mood between them quieted. Rucker knew that she meant her mother's early death from meningitis and her father's horrible accident in the private plane, but there was something else, too, something he'd learn one day when she was ready to talk. "This is too heavy a discussion before dinner," he teased gently. "Heavy food, heavy talk, whew! You want to be bloated?"

She looked up at him wryly. "You writers have such a charming way with words."

After dinner he turned the small console television in

the living room to a Saturday night game show and collapsed on the couch with his bare feet on her ottoman. Dinah harumphed audibly at his choice of entertainment, got a book from the nightstand in her bedroom, and returned to lie down with her head in his lap. He rested one big hand atop her right breast and caressed it from time to time.

"Comfortable?" she asked coyly. "Hand happy?"

"In heaven," he replied, and tweeked her nipple through the sheer material. Dinah smiled. Life with Rucker was a mellowing, sensual experience. He had wonderful, expressive hands that enjoyed touching, stroking, and massaging even when no sexual overture was involved. He had a way of conveying worlds of affection and comfort with those hands.

"What you readin'?" he asked. "Looks like more heavy stuff to me. Don't you ever read for fun?"

"I read the comics in the newspaper." She flipped a page in her paperback, lost in concentration. Suddenly his breast caressing hand turned traitor and whisked the book away from her. "Hey! Stop! Give that back!"

She sat up, reaching in vain for the book that he held just out of arm's reach. He grinned with malevolent glee. "Let's just peer at the back cover of this intellectual lookin' book." he told her. He began to read. 'Two-fisted adventurer . . . sexy, greed-crazed vixen . . . non-stop action . . .' Hmmmm, sounds like a date I had whilst I was in the army."

"Rucker, that book is complex science fiction."

"Let's just take a gander at the teaser on the inside page." Rucker cleared his throat, which ached with the need to laugh heartily. " 'Alexandra turned toward the huge android, her breasts heaving as she watched his unwavering approach. He wasn't flesh and blood, but her feminine instincts didn't notice that. "Zandrake," she hissed, "if you touch me, a Muluvian princess of the eighth order, I'll have my lieutenants turn you into a factory robonate." Zandrake took her in a fierce hold and crushed her to his chest. "For a few minutes of your pleasures," he growled in Muluvian trade lingo, "I'll risk that chance." ' "

Rucker clutched the book to his stomach and guffawed until tears slid out of his eyes. Smiling tightly, Dinah liberated her book and smacked him across the shoulder with it. "There's much more to it than that!" she protested.

"Zandrake!" he called in a high-pitched voice. "Zandrake, y'all take them nasty hands off my Muiuvian mounds before my daddy gets home from Mars, or he'll split your head like a bad watermelon!"

Dinah huffed with good-natured defeat and stretched out on the couch again. "It's a serious book," she protested smugly. "Be quiet."

"Aaah, Dee." Rucker's fingers sank into her loose, wavy hair and smoothed it tenderly. "You're full of surprises. I love it."

"Hmmm. Well, smart aleck, speaking of surprises, I happen to know that you have public TV shows on videotape. I found the collection the last time I was at your house. The tapes are hidden under your Willie Nelson albums." She counted on her fingers. "*Masterpiece Theatre, MacNeil/Lehrer NewsHour, American Playhouse, Nova*. Very impressive." She paused, suddenly sputtering on laughter. "*C-Captain K-Kangaroo—*"

"*Captain Kangaroo* is a classic!"

"*S-Sesame S-Street—*"

"*Sesame Street* is a classic too!"

"It's all right, big guy. You have great taste!" She sat up and kissed the embarrassed little smile on his mouth, then draped her arms around his neck and snuggled her face into the hollow of his shoulder. "Why didn't you want me to know that you watch serious television shows?" she asked softly. "Bad for your *Wheel of Fortune* image?"

"Yeah," he huffed. "And I don't like to look pretentious. Figured you'd think I was just tryin' to impress you."

"Oh, Rucker." She drew her head back and gazed at him tenderly. "You impress me, regardless."

He smiled, one of his big smiles that showed a nice row of blocky white teeth under his mustache. His hands splayed down her back and came to rest where it merged with the flare of her hips. "Read your silly old 'lust in space' book, and leave me be," he ordered sternly.

Dinah lay down again and got her book from the floor. "There's a nice wildlife special on PBS tonight," she prodded.

"I wanta watch the next show on this station first."

"There's a good movie on channel six."

"Oh, no, ladybug. I know your taste in movies. You think that if it ain't old and in black and white, it ain't worth watchin'. I like my movies with color."

"Blood and guts," she corrected wryly.

"Yeah. Red blood. Not black-and-white blood."

Her head pillowed on Rucker's thigh, Dinah became engrossed in her book again and tuned out the television audio. A few minutes later her concentration shattered when she heard, "And I'm Todd Norins bringing you the tragic story of a Montana woman who says visitors from another planet are behind the disappearance of her twelve children, her cat, and her Harley-Davidson motorcycle. Did state authorities cover the incident up? We'll tell you tonight, on *USA Personal*."

Dinah sat up swiftly, dislodging Rucker's hand from its cozy place inside the low-cut neck of her gown, and swiveled to look at the television. A handsome, though rather fleshy, face looked back at her with unforgettable coldness. Todd Norins had pale hazel eyes, eyes like an anemic hawk, she had decided long ago. His blond hair was carefully styled to appear thick in places where it was obviously thin. Her nostrils flared in disgust. Todd had gained weight and lost hair, but his eyes hadn't changed one iota. They still had the power to wrench her stomach. For years she'd managed to avoid seeing the man's face or hearing his voice. And now Rucker had brought him right into her living room. Why?

"You don't want to watch *USA Personal*, do you?" she asked in a wavering voice. "It gives journalism a very bad name."

"I know, I know," he admitted. Rucker pondered whether to mention his conversation with Todd Norins to her, but decided that he wouldn't. She'd just wonder why I was snooping, he told himself with a twinge of annoyance. "Relax," he coaxed, trailing the back of his hand across her cheek. She's turning pink, he noted with concern. Either she's embarrassed, mad at me for some reason I don't suspect, or upset at Todd Norins.

As she gazed, seemingly transfixed, at the television Rucker studied her expression closely. She purely dislikes Norins, he decided. What the hell did that sack of malarkey do to her years ago? The article he wrote had been complimentary and objective, so that wasn't the problem.

"I just wanted to see what makes this show so good," he told her.

"Lies and rumor," she said curtly. "Those always make a good show. Change the channel. This makes me sick."

"Why, Dee . . ." His voice trailed off, and he simply stared at her. He'd never heard that tone of voice from her before.

Rucker knew that part of Dinah's secrecy was tied to an old, deep-seated distrust of reporters, but this Norins situation didn't add up. Maybe—his chest tightened— maybe the Norins situation was personal. As in romantic.

"You know that guy?" Rucker asked casually, knowing that she did, of course.

"He wrote an article about me a long time ago. He covered the Miss America pageant for *Amazing World* magazine." She pointed to the screen. "Turn it to something else, Rucker."

Rucker's anxiety eased. If she'd denied knowing Norins, he didn't think he could have hidden his anger. "Bad article?"

She shook her head, her eyes never leaving the television. "Good article. Just basics." Her mouth curled in a hint of sarcasm. "I told him I wanted to change the world. Childish, idealistic hogwash like that."

"Not childish, Dee. Not hogwash." A commercial came on. Very subtlely, her shoulders sagged. She looked away from the television set, all the light and happiness gone out of her.

"Childish hogwash," she repeated. "And he knew it." She got up and wearily tossed her book on the hearth. "All right. Watch that trash if you want to. I'm tired. I think I'll go to bed."

Rucker stood up, studying her with a puzzled, worried frown. This sudden, moody retreat was totally unlike her. She didn't indulge in moods. That was one of the things he loved about her. "Am I invited along?" he asked grimly.

She didn't even look at him. "Do what you want."

He was amazed at the apathy in her voice. Rucker watched her glide down the hall toward the bedroom, her head lowered. Tension radiated from her like the shimmer around a candle. "Damn it, Dee," he whispered in distress, as if he were asking a question.

Rucker quickly checked the house for the night, shut Jethro in the kitchen with Nureyev, turned off the lights, then walked to the back of the house and entered the bedroom. She already had the lights off, and only a tiny, butter-yellow nightlight showed her shape under the bed covers. She lay on her side with her face turned away from the door. Away from the door and away from me, Rucker noted. He could almost feel her anguish, and it bewildered him.

Rucker undressed silently and slid into bed beside her. "Cold night," he whispered in a tone that forced lightness. "Good snugglin' weather." He moved close to her back, cupped himself to her spoon-style, and found her body as rigid as he'd expected. She still wore the creamy gown, and it gave him immense pleasure to know that she liked it.

Rucker sensed that his good taste had surprised her, and that she'd never hurt his feelings by saying so. He loved her for that too. She relaxed a fraction, shifting her body against his so that they were closely meshed. He knew then that she needed to communicate with him but was afraid to let her emotions go.

Rucker carefully curled his arm over her and unwound the hands she had burrowed against her chest. He held one of them, intertwining his fingers with hers and rubbing the back of her hand in slow, soothing circles. He nuzzled his face into her hair. "I'll let you keep some clothes on tonight," he teased gently. "I don't care if you're nekkid or not, long as I get to hold you."

She began to cry then, in a soft way that made barely any sound, and her fingers squeezed his fingers hard, as if she were trying to apologize for her odd mood. "Let it out, hon," he murmured, kissing her neck. "Whatever it is, just give it a good ol' cry."

She cried harder and, between gulps, managed to whisper, "You . . . have . . . the . . . best . . . voice in the world. And the best . . . touch."

"Rucker McClure, have voice and touch, will travel," he quipped softly. "Talk to me, hon. I don't know what's goin' on inside you, but I know you hurt like hell." His arm wound tighter around her. "Makes me hurt, too, you know."

"My father would have been sixty years old next week." Her voice was raspy and thick. "When the searchers found his plane, they . . . couldn't even tell who he was. Later, I went to see . . . for myself."

Rucker inhaled in sorrow and more puzzlement. What was it about Todd Norins that provoked this grief about her father? "Was that necessary, darlin'?"

"No. It was just something I had to do. It . . . I'll never forget . . . seeing him like that." She'd never forget the way Todd Norins had been waiting for her outside the morgue, either, but she couldn't tell Rucker that. "I was . . . so angry at Dad."

"Angry, hon?"

"Angry . . . because he was careless. The crash was due to careless error." Dinah felt raw fury surge through her, the old fury that she thought she'd learned to suppress. There was so much to be angry at her father for. Angry, confused, and bitterly disappointed. Hurting from the old wound, she began to pound the mattress with her fist, the action so fierce and uncontrolled that Rucker let go of the other hand and grabbed the violent one.

"Ssssh," he crooned, holding her balled fist. For a

second she struggled against him. "Dee!" he called in shock. She relaxed, almost whimpering.

"Rucker," she whispered sadly. "I'm s-sorry for being like this. I must seem so strange. . . ." Her voice rose. "I *hate* being at the mercy of other people!"

"You're not at my mercy, Dee," he answered, feeling hurt.

"Not you, sweetheart. Not you."

"Who, Dee? Todd Norins? Your father? Who?"

She was silent for several seconds, and Rucker realized that he'd reached the core of the old secret. The core, and the wall she'd built around it. "All right," he whispered. "You don't have to tell me . . . yet."

Several more seconds passed. "I can't talk about it now," she managed in a choking voice. "Someday I will."

"I'll be a-waitin'," he said with more cheerfulness than he felt. Her body, which had been cold and tense, now began to return to pliant warmth, and he sensed that she'd worked her crisis out, at least temporarily.

"I love you," she said firmly, and turning her face toward him, gave him a slow, gentle kiss. Rucker swept the tears off her face with his tongue.

"And I love you, possum queen." She laughed wearily and twisted around to snuggle deep inside his arms. "Just tell me one thing, Dee."

"Yes?" She sounded exhausted.

"Is Todd Norins somebody I should beat up on your account?"

"Rucker, you lovely Neanderthal, I don't want you to beat anyone up on my account. But you're awfully dear for wanting to. No other man has ever offered."

"This Todd Norins—"

"Don't." Her body stiffened with new tension. "No more. Let's just . . . go to sleep."

Rucker rocked her back and forth, cajoling her to relax, hiking the gown up to her hips and slipping his knee between her thighs to make his cajoling more effective. He had gotten no firm answer, but that was answer enough. Todd Norins, for some reason he didn't understand yet, was Dinah's enemy. And that makes the bastard my enemy, too, Rucker decided.

For a long time after Dinah fell asleep in his arms, Rucker lay awake worrying about the telephone conversation he and Norins had shared weeks ago.

Eight

The renowned chamber ensemble was well into Handel's Concerto Grosso in G Major, and Rucker was still out in the lobby looking for food. More precisely, a hot dog. As the violins swelled magnificently, Dinah exhaled in exasperation and began to rap her fingers on the upholstered arm of her seat. Bringing Rucker to the symphony was a mistake, she thought for perhaps the twentieth time. Unless the ensemble planned to sneak in a medley of Hank Williams hits, the evening was going to be a total loss.

Dinah could trace her love of the classics back to the parties her parents gave when she was growing up, glamorous parties where the men wore dinner jackets and the women were adorned in glittering, floor-length gowns. There had always been live music, always a small ensemble in the background playing classical pieces. She would slip, unseen, into the chandeliered living room and hide near the musicians, enthralled by the fairy-tale atmosphere. That mesmerized feeling came back to her when she attended concerts now, and she cherished it. She wanted Rucker to cherish it too.

Finally he returned, inching gracefully past the other people in the row of seats. The best row in the city's civic center, Dinah thought to herself, fuming. She'd paid a handsome price for these seats, and he'd better settle his lean fanny beside her and appreciate it. She watched as he smiled at everyone and they frowned back, annoyed by the disturbance. Well, the men frowned.

Dinah noticed that the women fluttered their eyelashes and checked Rucker over with great attention to detail. He did command admiration, despite the fact that he'd insisted on wearing a green cummerbund with a black tux. He reasoned that the cummerbund matched his eyes. Better a green cummerbund and a black tuxedo than a green tuxedo and a black cummerbund, she reminded herself. His height, his athletic build, that thick head of hair that reflected red and gold tones even in the low light, and that charming, mustached, "Hi, darlin' " smile added up to irresistible masculinity, Dinah admitted. But being gorgeous wouldn't save him now.

"What took you so long?" she whispered when he was finally ensconced next to her, one cowboy-booted foot propped on the opposite knee. "Is there a Bermuda triangle in the lobby?"

"I had to walk down the street to a convenience store," he said plaintively. "Nearly a quarter mile. Don't fuss at me. My feet hurt."

Dinah gaped at him in amazement. "You went outside this huge complex and walked a quarter of a mile in the cold, wearing a tuxedo, just to get a hot dog?"

"Not just any hot dog. A foot-long with extra pickle relish and pimento cheese." He leaned back comfortably and patted his stomach. "I'm ready for anything now. What're they gonna plunk out for the second half of the show?"

"The next piece is called 'Elgar's Serenade for Strings,' " Dinah muttered. She faced forward rigidly, aggravated with him.

"Sounds like a snappy tune. Who's Edgar?"

"Elgar, not Edgar. An English composer from the late nineteenth and early twentieth centuries."

"Another one of the dead ones," he sighed. "Aren't there any live ones writin' this stuff?"

Dinah closed her eyes in dismay. "Just be quiet and listen to it." Would anything good come out of this effort? During the piece, Rucker stretched his arm across the back of her seat and oh-so-casually brushed his fingertips along her bare shoulders, toying playfully with her heirloom pearl necklace as he did. Her dress was strapless, a luscious ball gown with a low, black velvet bodice and a billowing, pink taffeta skirt. Dinah straightened her back even more and ignored the cajoling touch. He inched his arm closer to her shoulders until it rested on them. The beautiful string music flowed around her as if it were Rucker's accomplice, coaxing her annoyance to fade.

After a few minutes she glanced at him from the corner of her eye. He was watching the ensemble, his expression relaxed and surprisingly content. Well, my goodness, Dinah noted, perhaps he's decided to give the classics a chance, after all. He shifted slightly, a big man in a small space, and flopped his arm over her shoulders so that his hand hung close to her right breast.

It was such a smooth and uncalculated act that Dinah didn't realize she'd been conned until his forefinger began to flick back and forth. He needed several seconds to locate her nipple under the black velvet that covered it, but once he accomplished his mission, his fingertip knew exactly what to do to make the traitorous peak swell.

Dinah cleared her throat, her face burning. She shifted, then shrugged hard and pushed at his hand. He removed it slowly, trailing his fingertips across the back of her neck, which was exposed by a curly, upswept hairstyle. His hand retreated to the arm of the seat.

Dinah leaned toward him. "Behave!" she intoned in a fierce whisper. "This isn't a drive-in!"

"Sssh!" an elderly gentleman hissed behind her.

Rucker looked down his nose at her with comical haughtiness. "Sssh," he echoed. Then, in a sly voice, one brow arching to emphasize his lack of repentance, "There are lots of ways to enjoy music, ladybug."

Dinah sighed in exasperation. So he'd show her how to enjoy music, would he? How very amusing. Suddenly his hand sidled over the arm of the seat onto her upper thigh. Dinah gasped and jumped, then quickly covered his indiscretion with her pink, richly patterned satin wrap. She looked at him, her eyes pleading.

"No," she mouthed. "Stop. I'll punch your lights out."

"Relax," he mouthed back, and smiled knowingly. Then he returned his attention to the musicians on stage. Dinah shifted in her chair, her heart pounding. This was outrageous! Under the satin wrap, her voluminous taffeta skirt and slip rustled as his expert fingers drew them up her legs. He wouldn't! she thought desperately. Even Rucker wouldn't . . . he *was*. And she couldn't make a scene. The last thing she wanted was to draw attention from the elegantly coiffed matron to the right of her. The woman would pop a diamond if she noticed what was happening.

And what was happening was that under the cover of her wrap, Rucker had her skirt and slip up to her thighs, and now he was stroking the sensitive skin on the inside of her legs. I should have known there'd be trouble when the man insisted that I wear a garter belt instead of panty hose, Dinah realized with shock. He planned this! Never in my life . . .

Dinah tapped her foot nervously, indicating that he must, simply must stop, but it was hopeless. His fingers slid under her black silk panties and dabbled playfully in the luxurious hair they found. Dinah bit her lip and glanced furtively at the woman beside her, who was, thankfully, very involved in the music.

Then she turned toward Rucker and shook her head authoritatively. "Stop it!" He winked at her, and his hand snuggled deep between her thighs. Breathing hard, she pulled the wrap further over her lap and tried to concentrate on the ensemble. She hadn't been raised as some prim southern debutante, but she had been taught decorum and precise etiquette. Dinah didn't think what Rucker was doing to her right now could even vaguely be classified as socially acceptable.

She shut her eyes and trembled with embarrassment as his fingers caressed areas where no gentleman's fingers had a right to be, in public. They sought the warm, soft folds of her body and stroked each one with great attention to detail. When his forefinger suddenly probed inside her, Dinah's eyes jerked open and she looked at Rucker in desperation. He was blithely watching the chamber ensemble, his face totally composed. But the color was dark in his cheeks, and his eyes were half shut. The knowledge that touching her had such an erotic effect on him made Dinah repress an involuntary sound of appreciation.

You rogue, she told him silently. You rake. You miscreant. You rascal. You redneck. You . . . you . . .

With a sigh, she settled back in her seat, trying to fight the hot, light sensation spreading through her body. She felt the sweet dampness that meant Rucker's ploy was working. She felt tendrils of excitement reaching out from her liquid center. She felt his fingers and thumb working in unison to make her ease her thighs apart. He succeeded. Dinah knotted one hand in her satin wrap and stared at the chamber ensemble.

"Elgar's Serenade for Strings" now qualified as the most erotic piece of music she'd ever heard. After it ended, the ensemble played Mozart's Divertimento in D Major, then Vivaldi's *The Four Seasons*, the final selection of the evening. Rucker continued his own concert, playing with amazing skill and perfect timing. Dinah kept her expression rigid and focused on the ensemble, never shifting her body, never giving in to the urge to arch her back and press forward into his hand. If I let myself go, she thought desperately, rustling taffeta will drown out the music. Perspiration gathered between her breasts, and she could feel every fiber of the velvet against her nipples.

Crescendo. She found new meaning in the term as the Vivaldi piece rose to a finish. Sensation crashed over her and through her, making her dip her head and close her eyes tightly, the manicured fingernails of one hand digging into her wrap, the fingernails of the other pressed deeply into a tiny gold purse she held. Rucker knew exactly what had happened, and afterwards he moved her panties back into place and caressed her over them. Good girl, his slow, gentle touch told her.

In a haze of shock Dinah didn't look at him. She was afraid she might simply sag against his shoulder with a satiated look of astonishment on her face, and immediately everyone would know their secret. He rearranged her slip and dress, patted her knee, then pulled his hand back into the polite confines of his own seat space.

She applauded the chamber ensemble numbly, biting her lip and occasionally touching one hand to her face, where the skin was fiery. The lights came up and she vaulted from her seat, trembling, and turned away from Rucker toward the aisle. She heard the soft sounds of his auditorium chair closing as he stood up, then felt his uneven breath on her neck.

"Sure would like to carry that purty pink shawl for you, ma'am," he intoned in a soft, throaty voice. "Sure would make me happy to do you that service. Put it right over my arm, hold it right in front of me, yep, sure would like to hold it in front of me, I sure would. . ."

"Here," she retorted in a squeaky tone, and thrust it over her shoulder.

His voice was droll and absurdly polite. "Thank you kindly, ma'am."

They made their way out of the row and melded with the crowd in the aisle. Dinah faced forward and kept her gaze on the black jacket of the man ahead of her. Rucker took her elbow with one hand. "It's awfully warm in here," she murmured, fanning herself, still not looking at him.

"Awful warm."

"Lovely concert."

"Dee-lightful."

She coughed, sputtered on restrained laughter, and twisted her head to gaze up at him, red faced. He looked back tenderly, then let go of her elbow and opened his arm in an invitation to her. Dinah stepped close to him, and his arm closed around her shoulders. She put her arm around his waist and hugged him.

"I'll never take you to a classical concert again," she promised.

The next week, he surprised her with a pair of season passes.

"Rucker, for heaven's sake! Am I going to have to wrestle with you right here in the mall? Now quit stalling!"

Rucker knew he looked defensive. Hell, I am defensive, he admitted. He gazed down at Dinah, who was tugging at his arm and grimacing with the effort. She wore her high-heeled boots, nice jeans, and a long, man's-style shirt in a soft blue plaid. A blue leather belt cinched it at the waist. A big canvas tote bag swung from her shoulder, she wore a leather coat, and her hair was done up in a loose bundle.

Beautiful turquoise jewelry accented the light blue of her eyes. As she pulled on his arm again a dark swirl of hair escaped and fell across her forehead. Rucker sighed. Even disheveled she was always flawlessly stylish and too adorable to resist. He squinted at the display window of the exclusive Birmingham men's store.

"I won't buy any colored underwear," he growled. "I draw the line at colored underwear."

"Who said anything about underwear!"

"You want to make me into a male model. They all wear colored underwear."

"My dear, deranged man, I just thought I'd help you improve your wardrobe. Isn't that what you asked me to do?"

"I recollect you simperin' sweetly at me over my grits this mornin' and saying, 'Why don't we go shopping today, sugar bunny?' Damn, I knew I was in trouble when I heard 'sugar bunny.' You're too dignified to call me 'sugar bunny' unless you really, really, want me to do something I don't want to do."

"You said that you'd like to get some new clothes!"

"New jeans! New . . . new crew socks! New golf shirts!"

"Rucker." She affected her most serious tone, the one he'd heard her use in city-council meetings when people got uppity. She emphasized each word. "You're

a famous writer. You speak to dozens of groups each
year. You're going to be interviewed on Larry King's
television show again soon. You need to look more
coordinated."

"Ugh. *Coordinated*. That's the word my house decorator used when she wanted to put cherubs everywhere."

"I promise I won't put a cherub on you."

Sighing, Rucker let her lead him into the store. It
was an elegant, darkly masculine place with dozens of
mannequins designed to look like stalwart, mature men.
"Hey," Rucker protested. "I don't want to shop anywhere where the dummies have gray hair! I'm not old."

"You won't live long enough to be old if you don't
pipe down. This is a store for executive types. Executive types are more likely to have gray hair. All right?"

"Yes'm," he grumbled.

A nattily dressed salesman hurried over. "May I help
you?" he asked in a supercilious tone, scanning Rucker's
barely laced jogging shoes, jeans with a torn knee,
college jersey, and blue hunter's coat. Annoyed, Rucker
started to say that he could help him by taking a
headfirst dive off a tall mannequin, but Dinah's dulcet
voice interrupted.

"My friend needs a whole new wardrobe," she said
politely. "For casual wear and for business. Colorwise, I
believe his best neutral is black. I think he'd enjoy
some low-keyed monochromatics, and as for combina-
tions, let's keep them analogous. Some blue schemes,
and green as well."

"Very good, very tasteful!" the salesman complimented.

Rucker turned to Dinah. "I don't have any idea what
you just told him I wanted."

She smiled at him sweetly. "You'll survive."

Rucker shook his head. He loved her more with each
new day, but he didn't know if he could put up with
being well dressed, much less monochromatic and analogous. For her, and her alone, he'd try.

Dinah sat in a darkly upholstered chair sipping a
glass of wine the salesman had given her. Her eyes
kept darting to the paneled door of the dressing suite.

When it opened suddenly, she nearly dropped her wine glass. Dinah set it down on a small lacquered table and stood up nervously.

The salesman stepped out smiling. He waved one hand toward the door and moved aside. "The gentleman has good raw material, thankfully," he noted.

The raw material walked out of the dressing suite wearing a classic navy blazer with dark gray slacks, a red tie accented with tiny, blue-and-white squares, and a white, button-down shirt with small, broadly spaced red pinstripes. The raw material looked at her anxiously, then tucked his chin and gazed down the length of his body. Dinah noticed that he wore black Italian loafers. With socks that matched, she presumed. It was an amazing transformation.

Rucker looked back up at her, studying her face with a plaintive gaze. "I look silly, Dee!" he exclaimed abruptly. The salesman blanched. "I can see it in your eyes!"

Dinah hurried forward, shaking her head. Rucker, for once in his life, was uncomfortable and uncertain. He had the desperate look of a horse about to bolt. "Big guy, you look fantastic," she reassured, clasping his hands.

He stared down at her, his green eyes narrowing to speculative slits. "Then why did you look at me that way!"

"What way?"

"Like I'm bad barbecue!"

"You're fine, just—"

"You can't put a rhinestone collar on a hound dog! I'm not right for chic clothes! People will point at me and say, 'There he goes, a rooster in eagle feathers!' No, Thanksgiving's too close. A turkey in eagle feathers—"

"Rucker, Rucker, calm down. You look wonderful." She stood back, gazing at him, her heart pattering with a thready beat. It was no flattery. She'd always appreciated well-dressed men, and the combination of stylish clothes with Rucker's natural sensuality was enough to make her press her hands to her throat and shake her head in stunned admiration. "Oh, honey," she sighed. "Oh, honey."

He kept studying her, and now he saw the happy glow in her eyes. Slowly, his cockiness returned. He looked down at himself again, held his hands out, and turned in a circle. "Pretty durned slick, then?"

"Pretty durned slick, you egomaniac."

"Very slick," the salesman agreed, relieved. "And this is just the beginning." He looked at Rucker warily. "Would you care for a glass of wine before we continue, sir?"

Rucker waved one hand and boomed, "Hell, get the whole bottle! I'm goin' on a shoppin' spree!"

Those words, *shopping spree*, sent the salesman hurrying off to fill the request. Dinah laughed as Rucker hugged her boisterously then lifted her off her feet and swung her in a circle. When he stopped she kisssed him on the nose.

"You think I look great," he said. "That's all I need to know. If you think I look great, then I know I look great." He paused, suffering another moment of indecision. "*Do* I look great, ladybug?"

Oh, to hell with my dignity, Dinah thought. She began to giggle and nod.

"Oooh, giggles. She's giggling! That's a good sign!"

"I'll make you a chart that will help you keep your new clothes matched correctly."

"What's to match? Men's clothes aren't like women's. We just put on what strikes our fancy."

She mimicked his drawl and lingo for effect. "I'm gonna strike your fancy—right upside your head." Dinah wagged a finger at him. "Dressing well is not as simple as you think. You have to keep the right colors and styles together."

He put her down and looked at her seriously. "I knew there was a catch," he intoned in a wry voice. The salesman came back with a full bottle of wine and a second glass. Rucker waved aside the glass, took the bottle, and swallowed a long swig straight from it. He squared his shoulders, eyed the salesman like a Marine about to charge into battle with a puny companion, and said, "Let's do it, buddy."

"Indeed." The salesman sniffed and led him away.

• • •

The weekly visit from a housekeeper kept Rucker's sumptuous, Early American bedroom sparkling clean and reasonably neat, but only a very brave housekeeper would attempt to navigate his walk-in closet. Apparently, Dinah thought with amused disgust as she surveyed it, no one has had that much courage. The closet, which was huge, had not one square inch of empty floor space. Old, partially strung tennis rackets hung from the clothes racks. A yellow, half-inflated river raft sagged against one wall. A collection of imported-beer bottles rested on the shoe racks.

Behind her, Rucker came trudging across the darkly carpeted bedroom floor, his arms stacked so high with his new purchases that he could barely see around them. "Outta my way," he puffed. "I got to put this stuff away before I get a hernia."

Dinah eyed him balefully. "Nothing new is going in this closet until everything old is removed." She studied the area, which was lit by a dim overhead light fixture. "I've counted twenty pairs of ancient jogging shoes, three moldy sets of golf clubs, six dilapidated pairs of golf shoes, and a five-gallon garbage bag full of dirty socks. Dirty socks, Rucker? Why?"

"I guess I forgot about 'em," he answered sheepishly. He went to his king-size bed and dumped all his bags and boxes on the dark spread. "I guess I thought the washing machine ate them. Washing machines have a way of doin' that, you know." He paused, then smiled at her rakishly. "Come on, Dee. Let's go downstairs and have a glass of wine in front of the fireplace. It's so cold and rainy outside, and I'd love to kiss your toes the way I did the other night. . . ."

"Not until we excavate the vault of 'Tutankhamen' McClure." Sniffing delicately, Dinah picked her way into the closet, kicked aside some jogging shoes, and sat down cross-legged. "Get a handful of garbage bags," she ordered. "The thirty-gallon size."

Mumbling about assertive women, he went downstairs and came back with the bags and a six-pack of cold beer. He sat down next to her on the floor, swallowed the contents of a can in three big gulps, then heaved the can over his shoulder. It landed neatly inside the upturned raft. "Two points," he noted cheerfully.

Dinah shoved his shoulder in mild rebuke, then opened one of the garbage bags and began stuffing shoes inside. "My memories," he said wistfully, watching her.

"Memories are not made of moldy athletic shoes."

"Aw, I guess you're right." He got a bag and began depositing shoes in it himself, without much enthusiasm. After a moment, he reached over to a cardboard box by the wall and pulled it toward him.

"What's that?" Dinah asked.

"My high-school yearbooks." He thumbed through one as she leaned toward him and peered curiously. "There I am." He pointed to a photo of the Latin Club.

"*You* were in the Latin Club?"

"Sure." He cleared his throat. "*Nunc est bibendum*," he said gravely. "That's a very serious Latin phrase."

She gave him an affectionate, but rebuking, look. "Of course it is. It means 'Now is the time for drinking.' "

He nodded. "Very serious."

Smiling, Dinah leaned forward and studied his picture. He was tall and awkward looking, just as he'd described to her once. All hands and feet and bony structure, like a coat rack waiting for the coat, and an angular face that showed strength of character but could not yet be called handsome. His hair was cut laughably short, even for twenty years ago. But it was the defiant look about him that drew her attention most: hands jammed in front pockets, legs braced, shoulders hunched. Even in the old photo it was easy to see the poverty behind his khaki work pants, baggy plaid shirt, and lace-up work boots. Her smile faded into sympathy.

"Uh, look pretty mean, there, don't I?" he said gruffly. "That picture was taken one afternoon right after school, and I was dreadin' work. From the time I was fourteen, I worked in a furniture factory afternoons and weekends. Summers too."

Dinah mentally compared her free time during the

highschool years: carefree, pampered days spent shopping, reading, and preparing for pageants. "You had to work, I suppose." she said softly. "There was no choice."

"Yep."

She touched the photograph with her fingertip and spoke softly. "A good kid."

"A bad kid," he corrected. "Believe it or not, I was sensitive. Too sensitive. I saw too many things wrong with the way people treated each other, so I used to fight . . . all the time. I'd get suspended, and my poor mama would come see the principal and repeat her same old story, bless her heart. 'He's not a bad boy. He's just not like anyone else, and they pick on him.' Good story. Kept me from endin' up in juvenile hall."

Dinah looked at him, open mouthed. This was a side of Rucker she'd never suspected. "I've always assumed that you were just like you are now—mellow."

His eyes were serious and somewhat bitter as he shook his head. "Kids who are dirt poor have a hard time bein' mellow. It's humiliating to wear your father's hand-me-downs and never have enough money to buy a full lunch in the school cafeteria. Especially in a small town, where everybody knows that you're poor and your father was no-account."

"He was?"

"Chased everything in skirts. Had such bad credit that nobody'd even loan him a pot to—well, nobody would loan him anything."

"Oh, Rucker." She stroked his arm.

"I was glad when the mean bastard died in that truck accident. Real glad. But I had to wear his damned leftover clothes until I went into the Army. As soon as I got my army issue I threw away every piece of his clothes."

Dinah shoved the garbage bags aside and scooted over to put her arms around Rucker's neck. She kissed him. "I'm glad you're not like everybody else." She kissed him again. "So it's good to have new clothes?"

He smiled a little. "Uh-huh. It's like puttin' the past behind you. I always feel that way about new clothes."

"Really? I didn't make you buy things you hate?"

"Nope." He sighed grandly, looking resigned. "It's time to move into the next phase of my life. The *Esquire* phase."

"*Esquire*, my foot. I don't want an *Esquire* man." Her voice dropped. "I want you." Dinah began to pull him down, pushing old jogging shoes aside as she did. She felt such tenderness for him after what he'd just told her about his youth that she wanted to love the sadness out of him. "Right here, right now."

"Here?" He gestured around them. "Near the dirty socks? Dee? Are you sure you feel okay?"

"Yes." She began pulling up his sweater, his new sweater, a muted blue with fine gray and white stripes. He wore it over an oyster-gray shirt, the collar peaking stylishly over the sweater's neck. He had on crisp new jeans. "I prefer your old jeans," she whispered huskily, as he stretched out beside her. "They're more . . . uhmmm . . ."

"Form fittin'," he said devilishly. "I know how you like to watch my form."

"I do like to watch you. I admit it."

He unbuttoned her blousey plaid shirt and slid his hand inside to cup one of her breasts over the lacy bra she wore. "Dee," he whispered. "I never thought you'd want to make love to me on top of old jogging shoes. You sure have gotten earthy."

"I'd make love to you anywhere, big guy."

He took her in his arms and his eyes filled with devotion. "This relationship of ours is working out just as well as I figured, ladybug. We're definitely compatible. Like hot corn and cool butter." He lowered his head and began kissing her neck. "I love you, butter."

She nodded, smiling at his silly analogy but feeling strange, as if she might cry from a mixture of conflicting emotions. She still had the dismal fear that the future wouldn't be as wonderful as the present. "I love you, corn," she whispered.

It was an unusually cold afternoon for early December, and a white mountain fog had rolled in early, bringing with it a fine mist that just stopped short of

qualifying as rain. Dinah liked this kind of weather—
"toast and tea weather," as Rucker called it. It made
everything indoors feel so cozy and warm. Even her
small mayor's office with its scarred, corkboard walls,
battered desk, and humming space heater seemed cheerful. Outside, the first shades of dusk were drawing
around Mount Pleasant even though the courthouse
clock had only just finished striking five.

Dinah sipped a mug of coffee and bent over the neat
stack of paperwork on her desk. She reached out and
adjusted the jointed arm on the drafting light that was
screwed to one corner of the desk, pulling the light
closer to her. As she did, she heard the click of the
phone intercom. Lula Belle's voice came out.

"Rucker's on line one." She chortled. "He asked me
why I was workin' late instead of chasin' men. I told
him I've got enough trouble figurin' out city water bills."

Dinah laughed. "After what we went through today, I
don't think we'll ever get them straight." She punched
a button on the phone console. "Flirting with the city
clerk won't get you anywhere, sir."

"Oh?" Even long-distance, his deep voice sent pleasant shivers up her spine. "Who do I have to flirt with to
get satisfaction?"

"The mayor."

"You mean that beautiful brunette who has such
good taste in men?"

"I'm afraid she doesn't look beautiful today. She looks
a bit soggy. She's been outside trying to trace a lost
water line."

"Don't y'all have a map of those things?"

"Well, you would think so, wouldn't you? My prede-
cessor, the honorable Mervin Flortney, lost it. Odd, but
his house is on the mystery water line. Hasn't paid a
water bill in years." Dinah adopted a Sherlock Holmes
voice. "Fascinating, wouldn't you say, Watson? Makes
one wonder if the loss was intentional, eh?"

"Eh. Does a hound dog have fleas?"

"Precisely. At any rate, Lula Belle and I have just
spent two hours tracking down water valves on West
Pleasant Road. I'm sitting here with mascara smeared

under my eyes and an old towel on my head, wearing dirty jeans and a damp sweatshirt. One of your old ones."

"Why, how disgustin'," he said primly. "I'm wearin' a dress shirt—something in a pale robin's-egg blue, my best color—a charming, tan silk paisley tie, and exquisitely tailored tan slacks."

"Why, how nice," she answered drolly. "You got the chart right, for once. You certainly must look like the top turnip in the patch, Mr. Turnip Head."

"Mean politician."

They both chuckled. "So how's Dallas?" she asked. "Are you ready to give your speech?"

"Dallas is great! You ain't gonna believe the suite these cattlemen got for me. It's at this old grand hotel named The Adolphus. It's got antiques in it. I don't know whether to sit on the bed or take a picture of it. This is the suite Jimmy Carter stays in when he comes to Dallas on business. How about that?"

"You're a VIP," she said, smiling. "Give me your room number."

"It's a suite," he protested with mock rebuke. "A suite, not a room." He relayed the number, and she wrote it down. "I'll give you a call tonight, ladybug, after we get through. I gotta run 'cause the Gannon boys want to buy me a couple of drinks before dinner."

"The Gannons? As in Gannon International?"

"Just a few of my associates," he sighed with great nonchalance. "You know how it is for us slick-dressed people. A beer with the jet-setters, prime rib with the cattlemen's association, a speech that knocks them on their horns a-laughin' . . ."

"A wildly inflated self-assessment," she replied tartly. "Call me later, you handsome hound. I love you."

His voice became soft and serious. "I love you too. And tell Jethro that Daddy says hello."

"He'll be so thrilled. Since his expression never changes, I won't be able to tell that he's thrilled, but I'll assume that he is."

Rucker was still laughing when he said good-bye. Dinah hung up the phone and sat without moving for a while, thinking about him and smiling. She was so lost in daydreams that at first she didn't hear the new voices in the hall outside her office. When she realized that Lula Belle was arguing with someone loudly—and loudly was loud, with Lula Belle—Dinah leapt up and hurried toward the door.

"You get out of here!" she heard Lula Belle screech. "All right, then, *all right*! I'm callin' the police!"

A sudden sinking sensation, part fear, part foreboding, grabbed at Dinah's stomach. As she reached her door a man blocked her way. Dinah halted, her heart freezing, her hands rising involuntarily to her throat as if to protect it. Pale, predatory eyes gleamed down at her. Todd Norins held out a hand with well-manicured nails.

"It's certainly nice to see you again, Dinah. After all these years." He almost smiled.

Nine

It had been a good night, a good speech, and a good time, Rucker thought contentedly as he leaned against the beveled glass of the private penthouse elevator. In recent years, success had lived up to all its promises, and he was a happy beneficiary. Rucker puffed a cloud of fragrant smoke from a long cigar. He enjoyed smoking a good cigar sometimes, and this one was magnificent.

Humming an old Tammy Wynette song, he straightened as the elevator reached his floor. The door slid back with the graceful whoosh of fine machinery, and Rucker stepped into a small lobby decorated in Queen Anne antiques, the fabrics flowery, the ambience elegant and old-world. Rudolph Valentino had once stayed in this hotel. And John Wayne. Can't picture the Duke among all this frippery, Rucker thought sternly. Fumbling with his hotel key, he climbed a winding, private staircase that led up one story to the landing of his exclusive suite.

The sight of Dinah seated on the floor, her back against the suite's door jamb, brought him to an astonished stop. She uncurled her long legs and got up slowly, her movements awkward and weary.

"Dee!" he called, and covered the last few steps in one leap. He threw the cigar into an ash stand by the door and grabbed her shoulders. Rucker stared down at her, fear and concern twisting his stomach. She looked like she'd been through hell. "What is it, hon? What are you doin' here?"

Her voice was hollow and cold. "The game's over. Drop the southern comfort act, Rucker. I know what you really want from me now."

Shock left him speechless for once in his life. He blankly noted that her glorious dark hair, usually so perfect, now hung in limp, disheveled strands, as if she'd spent hours running her hands through it. She wore her leather coat over the floppy gray sweatshirt and dirty jeans. Her feet were covered by mud-stained tennis shoes, and a small leather purse dangled from the angry fist her right hand made. That fist drew his attention.

"Punch me or explain what's wrong," he ordered desperately. Her face was what upset him most. It was swollen from crying, and now her eyes glittered with new tears. New tears, exhaustion, and bitterness, as she gazed up at him mutely. Bitterness he couldn't comprehend.

"I wanted to believe in you so badly," she said in a dull voice. "Don't you have any shame?"

"Dee? What the hell is the matter? What happened? Why'd you fly to Dallas?" He tried to take her in his arms, but her hands came up and braced against his dark blue jacket. She held him away, and he gazed down at her in utter bewilderment, frowning.

"We have to talk," she said, and her icy tone cut through him. "I don't want your sympathy. I want explanations."

"What *is* it?" he demanded, his fear making him so reckless that he shook her slightly. "Damn it, Dee, tell me!"

"Let go of me!" She shoved him fiercely, and he was so amazed that he released her arms. She stepped back, her chest moving harshly as she took quick, short breaths. "Stop pretending to be innocent! I hate this act of yours!"

"*Dee*?" he said again, stunned. She was a stranger, a violent stranger blind with fury. "What the—"

"What did Todd Norins promise you?" Her voice was cutting. "A plug on his show for your books or your column? That he'd help you get some spectacular job in broadcasting? That he'd share the credit when he broke my story? What, Rucker? What would make me worth all the trouble you went through? Seduction *and* courtship. I must be one hell of a good story to you!"

The sound of Norins's name had startled him, and now he looked down at her in new silence as a terrible sense of understanding crept over him. "Oh, no," he groaned.

"He showed up at my office today. He brought his *cameraman* along." Her voice was full of sarcasm. "We had an impromptu *interview*. It consisted mainly of Norins asking me *questions* and me telling him to *get out*. The tape will be aired in all its glory on *USA Personal* next week." She paused, her eyes glinting even brighter. "He said you told him where to find me." Her voice broke as tears streamed down her cheeks. "You told . . . told him everything . . . you knew about me. Why, damn it? What was the payoff for you! That's all I want to know! What was the payoff!"

Shaking his head, he took a step toward her, his hands out in supplication. "Dee, it wasn't like that, I swear. I never tried to hurt you. I was looking for information. I called Norins because he'd done that article years ago—"

"Looking for information that would flesh out your own story?" Her voice rose. "After you told me that you'd leave my past alone until I was ready to discuss it!"

Anger invaded Rucker's emotions. "Damn it! Why can't you trust me!" He felt bad enough without being accused of motives he'd never had. "I called Norins after we spent the night together that first time," he told her grimly. "I was trying to find out what you were hiding so I could break down all those damned barriers you put up."

"You told him where to find me!" she yelled, her hands gripping his lapels suddenly. She jerked at them. "How *could* you! I don't believe your explanations! I want the truth!" Her cheeks were flushed a bright red, contrasting markedly with the pallor of her face.

"Stop it," he ordered. "You're just about hysterical.

Damn it, I'm innocent! I didn't have any ulterior motives."

"You didn't have any ulterior motives," she repeated sardonically. "Thank you. That's grand. Everything I've worked to build is—" she dipped her head and fought to continue speaking, "is ruined. But you're innocent. Wonderful." She let go of him and backed away. "A great story, Rucker."

He'd had enough. Rucker stepped past her and unlocked the door to the suite. He slung it open and grabbed her by the wrist. "Get in here," he told her. "I won't have everybody who walks into the lobby below us listenin' to this garbage. I'm gonna put you into bed and order you a double shot of bourbon. Then I'm gonna talk some sense into you and get some explanations."

"And make everything better?" she asked tautly. "Don't try to cajole me with your down-home domestic charms. Nothing is going to get better—"

"Nothin' is goin' to get better until you explain about Norins!" He stepped into the suite, pulled her in behind him, and slammed the door shut. "Talk!"

"I don't owe you any answers." She tugged her hand away furiously.

He looked as if he might explode with anger and frustration. "I *love* you, despite what you think, Dee. You owe me."

The sound of those words, *I love you*, crumbled her defenses. She hurried across an elegantly appointed living room to a huge skylight that filled one slanted wall. She stood there framed by the glittering panorama of Dallas at night, her face buried in her hands, her back to him. Rucker thought he'd die if he didn't at least try to touch her.

He walked up behind her without a word and slid both arms around her waist, then hugged her tightly and rested his cheek against her disheveled hair. She was pure resistance, tense and trembling.

"Tell it all," he said in a gravelly voice. "Please. Whatever the hell it is, or was, that hurts you so much, tell me right now."

"Let go of me. I don't want you to hold me. I trusted you, and you destroyed that trust."

"You've *never* trusted me." He was so angry and hurt that he had trouble getting the words out. "Why should now be any different?" Her shoulders sagged, and he knew he'd made his point. His voice became less harsh. "Dee. I called Norins to ask questions about you. When he asked questions in return, I didn't know it would cause trouble to answer them. I didn't *know*. Don't hate me for makin' a mistake. You're the center of my life, and I'd do anything to keep from hurtin' you. Can't you trust me a little, and believe that? Don't hate me. Don't . . . hate . . ." He stopped, unable to go on.

She sobbed quietly and took several seconds to get her voice to a point where she could speak again. "I don't hate you. Please . . . just let go of me. I . . . you're confusing me. It makes it harder to talk."

"There's nothing to be confused about. I'm not in cahoots with Norins." His voice was a graveled whisper. "I couldn't hurt you, Dee. It would be like hurting myself."

"I don't know what to believe. It doesn't . . . matter. Nothing matters, anymore. He found me. He found out about me."

Feeling empty and cold inside, Rucker moved leadenly to a dark, patterned couch and sat down. Dinah raised her head and stared out at the crystalline, wintry lights of the night skyline. "Talk," he said curtly. "Give me something, Dee. I have to know what you've been hidin' all these years."

She struggled for a moment. Then she took a deep breath. "My father was president of a large banking firm."

"I know. It's one of the few things you've told me about him."

"My father,"—she hesitated, nearly choking—"was, according to a great deal of evidence, a thief and a liar."

Stunned, Rucker studied her quivering back and knew that she'd just made one of the most difficult statements of her life.

"Right before his death," she continued slowly, "he was about to be indicted by a federal grand jury for embezzling, fraud, and money laundering . . . involving twenty-five million dollars. And I . . . was suspected of knowing all about his activities. And deliberately concealing them."

As long seconds passed neither of them spoke. Then Rucker said in a pensive tone, "And not long before the Miss America pageant, Norins got on the trail of that story."

She nodded, and her whole body trembled. Rucker vaulted to his feet. "Are you all right?"

"Yes." She held up a reassuring hand. "Don't . . . don't come over. I'm fine." She hugged herself tightly. "When Dad's plane crashed, he was carrying some important pieces of evidence—transactions—on board. They had been subpoenaed by a grand jury. Of course, without them, and without his testimony, there wasn't much . . . of a case for the prosecution. And all but five million dollars of the money was recovered after he died."

"Oh, Dee."

"You sound sympathetic," she noted without emotion. "I assume that means that you think I was innocent."

He strove not to grab an antique oriental vase off a nearby end table and throw it against the wall in frustration. "Of course I think you were innocent. I know you as well as I know myself."

"I wasn't innocent."

"*What*?"

"I wasn't innocent." She turned to face him, her hands clasped in front of her, her face ashen, her eyes dazed. She looks like she's waiting to be executed, Rucker thought. "I knew my father was involved in something illegal. I tried to talk to him about it, but he kept assuring me that nothing was as it seemed. And I believed him. He had always been the most honorable, the most idealistic . . . ." She cleared her throat roughly. "When investigators began to come to me on the side, asking questions, I . . . lied like a good daughter. So, I did conceal evidence."

"Honey, there's nothing wrong with tryin' to protect somebody you love."

"He . . . died in the Cessna crash . . . and afterward the investigators traced part of the embezzled money to an old savings account he and Mom started for me when I was a baby." She waved one hand weakly. "He'd put stolen money in my name. I couldn't believe . . . that my adoring father would voluntarily do something that might jeopardize me. But he did. Ironic, isn't it." She swayed, and Rucker moved toward her anxiously. "Ironic, that I thought he was so wonderful . . . and it was all . . . a lie."

Her legs wilted under her, her head tilted back, and she sank bonelessly toward the floor. Rucker caught her just before she hit. "Dinah!" he said urgently as he picked her up and carried her down a hallway to the suite's richly decorated bedroom. He placed her on a canopied, four-poster bed and ran to the bathroom. By the time he returned with a damp washcloth, she was trying to sit up.

"No way. Back down," he ordered in a worried voice. He gently pushed her flat again and arranged a big pillow under her head, then sat down beside her and wiped her face with the cool cloth. "You've made yourself sick, dammit. Lay still."

She looked up at him with exhausted, apathetic eyes. "Norins learned—"

"I don't care. You need to rest." He was almost begging her.

"No! Norins learned, when he was covering the Miss America contestants, enough to know something suspicious was going on with me. He told me that if I won the title . . . that he wouldn't stop until he got the story, because if I were Miss America a scandal would be big news." She exhaled roughly and new tears slid from the corners of her eyes. Frowning, Rucker wiped them away with his fingertips. "Miss America, an accomplice in one of the biggest embezzlement schemes in the history of banking. A great story, and a Norins exclusive. I still have nightmares about the public persecution he'd have put me through if I'd won the title."

"But all you did was protect your father."

"I lied to federal investigators. I just knew that if Dad said he was innocent, then he was innocent." She closed her eyes. "A few weeks after I dropped out of the pageant, a formal charge was made against me. Concealing illegal activities. Maximum sentence, three years, or a five-hundred-dollar fine. The trial was all very hushed up. The bank didn't want publicity. It would have looked bad, since they had no idea where to find the last five million dollars."

Rucker gazed at her in astonishment for a moment, the world *trial* making a sick buzz in his ears. He pictured her going through all the torment of it alone, her pride and her innate dignity being challenged at every point. He tried to speak with a casual tone that belied his heartache. "So you paid the fine."

She opened her eyes slowly and looked up at him. Rucker's stomach twisted as he saw the shame and pain clouding their delicate blue. "Nothin' bad about a fine," he murmured desperately. "That's all it was, then. A fine?" Please God, he prayed silently. For her sake, that's all it was.

Her wretched voice tore at him. "I was sentenced to three years in prison." Horror crawled up his spine and he was dimly aware that tears came to his eyes. *No, Dee, oh, no. I love you too much to bear what you're going to say next.* "I served one year."

Dinah watched grief pour into his expression. He winced sharply, turned his head, and shut his eyes. His hands clenched and unclenched rhythmically. "Rucker?" she whispered hoarsely. He drew deep breaths.

"Give me a second."

"I've always been terrified that when I told you . . . about prison . . . that you'd be ashamed of me. Are you?"

"Ashamed?" His voice was barely audible. "No!" Something broke inside him. He clasped her shoulders hard and shook his head. Slowly, tears slid down his face. He made a gruff sound of anguish, bent over her, and rested his head against her shoulder.

He's crying for me, Dinah thought in shock. She turned her face so that her lips were against his ear, and her tears mingled with his. Rucker was the kind of man who never cried, who considered crying a mortal embarrassment. And yet here he was, crying without reserve, on her behalf. Her previous anger and accusations died in a wave of devotion. Dinah stroked the back of his head with quick, almost frantic, hands.

"I love you so much," she murmured brokenly. "Sssh."

"Damn it, it wasn't fair."

"Stop, stop," she begged. "It was bearable. Dad had important friends who made sure of . . . that. I went to California, stayed at a minimum security prison . . . a country club sort of place." She tried to make a joke, to ease Rucker's anguish. "I met so many interesting politicians and business executives . . ."

But his body shook harder, though he made no sound. His fingers dug harshly into her coat. "Sweetheart," she murmured. "Sweetheart, don't." Finally, he uttered a long stream of obscenities that ended with a fierce "Damn the whole freakin' world for doin' that to you."

"Sssh, sssh." Aching because she loved him so much and didn't want him to hurt for her this way, Dinah put her arms around his back and held him. After a minute he got himself under control and his grip on her shoulders relaxed a little. He raised his head and looked at her sadly. "Tell me the rest," he said.

Dinah cleared her throat. "Norins forgot about me after I dropped out of the pageant. He was distracted. The television people had just offered him the spot on *USA Personal*. But I've always been afraid that he'd wonder what became of me . . . that some day he'd begin to nose around . . ."

"And I led him straight to you. How much does he know?"

"Everything. I suspect that he found someone who served on the bank's board of directors when my father was president. Dad made enemies on the board because he had a way of pinpointing incompetence." Her voice grew sarcastic. "He was an exemplary leader, except for being an embezzler."

Rucker squeezed her arm in sympathy. "Norins," he reminded her gently. "What did he ask you about today?"

Distress replaced the sarcasm in her tone. "He asked me whether I felt that being a convicted criminal jeopardized my credibility as a mayor and school teacher. Why hadn't I told the school board and the voters about myself. Things like that."

"Say good-bye to Miss American Pie. That's his angle, then, the jackass."

"He's going to paint me as someone who deceived a little Bible-Belt town into believing that I'm respectable." She gripped Rucker's shoulders. "He wants people to believe that I've got the missing five million dollars hidden somewhere! He'll make everyone in Mount Pleasant look like gullible fools for trusting me!"

"Sssh. Everything will be all right." His confidence amazed her and grated on her overwrought nerves.

"How can you say that?" She tried to sit up, but he put a hand on her shoulder and held her down. "Don't say that to me!"

"You're free now, Dee. Your past doesn't have a hold on you anymore. That's good." He kissed her and got up, then stood beside the bed, looking down at her with a solemn gaze. He seemed desperate to pretend that everything was wonderful again, as if she hadn't just told him that she'd spent a year in prison. "No more talk tonight, ladybug. Come on. I'll help you get undressed. Then I'm going to order room service for you. I bet you haven't eaten since—"

"Rucker! Don't stand there trying to make me forget what's happened! It won't work! Just stop glossing everything over. I know you feel guilty, but don't pretend that my life is going to be better because of what you did!"

Slowly, the color rose in his cheeks, and his jaw tightened. "I told you that I was sorry for tipping Norins off. Are you gonna keep blamin' me?"

They shared a tense look laden with communication. She didn't want to speak the words, and she didn't have to. He read the answer in her regretful but unyielding eyes.

"I love you," she told him, "and I know that you didn't mean any harm by telling Norins about me . . . but, yes . . ."

"But, yes, you did screw up my life, Rucker," he supplied angrily. "I think I did you a favor by gettin' this mess out in the open."

"A favor!"

"You won't be haunted anymore. You'll go on with your job and your political career—"

"I have no political career."

"Oh, yes, you do, little lady." The way he used *little lady* told Dinah that he expected her to do as he said. "You're gonna run for state senate, just the way you've always intended."

"No one is going to vote for an ex-con."

"Oh, hell, we're into self-pity now, are we?"

Dinah sat up rigidly, feeling embarrassed, mad, and defensive. "No, not self-pity. Dignity. Pride. The desire to lead a life free from whispers and innuendo."

"You've got to have more faith in people."

"Pardon me, but I lost a large measure of my faith in people six years ago, starting with my father."

"Maybe your old man was innocent."

Dinah got off the bed and faced him with a tired but imperious stance. "I wish I had your appealingly simplistic view of life."

"My dumb, *countrified* view of life," he retorted. "Isn't that what you mean, snob?"

Her face flamed with anxiety and anger, but she made her voice sound businesslike. "I have to get back to the airport. Tomorrow's going to be a long, unpleasant day. I'll call you."

She started to go around him, but he blocked her way. Rucker looked down at her with a stern expression. "You're half-sick and upset. Just forget about prissing out of here tonight."

Prissing? The derogatory description made another dent in her badly battered control. "Get out of my way," she demanded.

"No. If you want to dislike me and blame me for what's wrong in your life tonight, fine. But you're gonna get undressed, get in bed, have some dinner, and go to sleep. I'll go back to Mount Pleasant with you in the morning."

"I want to go now. It's my problem. I'll handle it alone." She took another step. Again he blocked it. Dinah stared up at him in fury and consternation, at a loss for ways to deal with his macho, authoritative attitude.

"It's our problem," he told her. "Don't let pride make a fool of you. You're not goin' anywhere tonight. That's final."

Dinah could feel rebellious urges gathering inside her. "I don't like your Clint Eastwood persona," she answered stiffly. "I'm not like the other women you've known. I won't put up with the old male-dominance routine."

She waited for him to move. He didn't. When he spoke, every word was slow and emphasized. "Either you quit arguing and stay voluntarily," he said, "or I tie you up. I swear I'll do it, for your own good."

Dinah's hands rose to her throat in a gesture of disbelief. "That's ridiculous." Her eyes glittering with challenge, she stepped around him and walked down the hallway. She heard Rucker start after her. She heard the rustling of cloth. She heard his gruff, "I warned you, dammit."

Dinah swung around. "Oh, Rucker, don't make absurd threats—" He grabbed one of her arms and looped his silk tie around the wrist before she could withdraw. "Rucker, no!" Dinah jerked hard against the makeshift bond and only succeeded in pulling it snug.

"Change your mind and stay voluntarily," he ordered. "I'm not above hogtiein' you."

She snatched at the knotted silk with her fingertips. "Get this off me!"

His hands moved as if he was going to comply, and she was caught off guard when he snaked the tie around her other wrist. "This isn't funny!" she protested bitterly, trying to move away from him. He pushed her against a wall and held her there with the pressure of his body. Dinah squirmed desperately.

"I think it's real funny," he noted angrily. "The big, bad redneck is takin' the snob prisoner."

"Rucker. *Rucker!*"

Once he had her hands tied firmly, he hoisted her into his arms and carried her back into the dimly lit bedroom. Dinah was so furious that she gulped staccato breaths. He laid her on the big, ornate bed and pulled her arms above her head. "Last chance," he noted, his voice grim. "I'll untie you if you'll give me your word that you'll stay put."

"No!" she said between clenched teeth. Tears of frustration ran down her face. "I want to see if you'll really go through with it!"

He nodded brusquely. "Oh, yes ma'am, I will." Then he tied her hands to the bed post. Dinah drummed her heels into the bedspread while he calmly said, "Let's get these dirty shoes and jeans off you."

She stared at him in silence as he calmly removed her shoes, socks, and finally, the grimy jeans. He eyed what remained, her blue silk panties, the sweatshirt, and her leather coat. "Hmmm. A technical problem I can't solve. Guess you'll have to keep the sweatshirt and coat on." But he slid his hand under the shirt, found the front clasp on her bra, and flicked it open. "There. How's that? More comfortable?"

Humiliated and mad, she turned her face away and refused to answer. He bent over her, his breath brushing her face as he worked the bedspread and sheets out from under her. He covered her with their downy warmth and arranged the pillows under her head. Then he went to the bed's opposite side, sat down, and picked up the telephone on a small nightstand.

Dinah hardly listened as he called room service. She realized suddenly that she was too exhausted to fight him, too exhausted to care about this outrageous tactic of his or the problems she'd face tomorrow at home. She grew still as her tense muscles responded to the incredibly comfortable mattress and luxurious sheets. The room was cozy, lit only by a small bedside lamp. When Rucker got off the phone he glanced at her then went into the bathroom and returned with a fresh washcloth.

Dinah squinted her eyes shut. She didn't open them when he began wiping her swollen face, or even when he gently took her chin and turned her face toward him for better access. "Come on, Dee," he urged in a tired voice. "Give in."

Give in reactivated her resistance. "You like me tied up, you keep me tied up," she answered.

"Hellion," he muttered without much conviction. He tossed the covers aside and ran the washcloth over her legs and feet. "You've got a blister on your heel. From all that walkin' you and Lula Belle did today?"

She decided that silence was her only retaliation. When she didn't answer, he bent over her foot and kissed the blister, his mustache tickling. "Sorry about your foot," he whispered. "Sorry about Norins. Sorry about fighting with you. Sorry about tyin' you up." He rested his cheek against her ankle, and a traitorously tender feeling filled her chest. He covered her up, then went to retrieve the purse she'd dropped on the floor when she collapsed.

Like the living room, the bedroom had a floor-to-ceiling window covered in narrow blinds. In front of the window was a sitting area. Rucker went there and unceremoniously dumped the contents of her purse on the coffee table. Dinah raised her head to stare at him curiously but squelched the urge to demand an explanation. He found her hairbrush, went to his suitcase, and pulled the lace out of one of his jogging shoes.

"You'll feel happier when your hair's fixed up," he assured her when he came back to the bed. He sat down beside her, arranged her hair on the pillow, and began to brush it using long, careful strokes. After her initial disbelief wore off, Dinah sighed in distress. His touch, as usual, was wonderful. She gave in a little.

"My hair is the least of my problems," she told him.

"I know you," he insisted. "You aren't comfortable if your hair is all messy."

He pulled it into a swathe that lay on her shoulder, then spent twenty minutes trying to form that swathe into a braid. Finally he proclaimed the result, "exquisite, if I do say so my own self," and tied it with his shoe lace. He got a hand mirror out of the bathroom and held it up for her to look. Dinah didn't want to look, but she couldn't help herself. Only Rucker Mc-Clure would tie a woman to a bed, then act as if nothing extraordinary was happening.

She looked. The braid was unsymmetrical, and little loops of hair stuck out all over it. "Hmmmph."

"Thank you."

There was a knock at the suite's door and he strode out, shutting the bedroom door behind him. I should scream, Dinah thought with weary humor. That would serve him right. Let him try to explain to the waiter why he has a woman tied to his bed. She tucked her chin and looked at herself. A woman who's still wearing a coat and a floppy sweatshirt. She tested her wrists against the soft silk of his tie, and flexed her arms. Hog-tied.

Rucker came back with an overloaded tray, which he set in the middle of the bed. He sat cross-legged beside it and fed her. She stared straight ahead and accepted each mouthful with cold silence. "Guess you're grateful that I ordered all your favorite stuff," he noted hopefully. Dinah looked at the odd assortment and couldn't help feeling touched. Fettucini Alfredo, chocolate ice cream, clam chowder, and a chicken salad sandwich. Since she liked Burgundy wine best of all, he'd ordered that, too, heedless of compatibility.

After he cleared the dishes away he switched off the lamp and undressed in the dark, tossing his clothes onto the floor. Dinah couldn't stand that. "Hang your jacket and slacks up!" She heard his rich, soft chuckle and realized that she'd been duped.

"I knew that would get you to talk!" he drawled. He got into bed and immediately slid over to her. Burning with new annoyance, Dinah turned her face away and shut her eyes as he pressed close to her side. He was naked.

"Howdy," he drawled. He nestled one long, hairy leg between her thighs, rested his head on her shoulder, and slid one hand under her sweatshirt. He casually spread it, palm down, just beneath her rib cage. "Cold hand," he explained coyly. "Needs a warm spot."

The tentative, playful mood was a sham, and they both knew it. Lying there in the dark, the silver glow from the city lights sifting over them through the skylight window, they were enveloped in sorrow. Dinah quivered as Rucker's thumb traced small circles on her bare stomach.

"You win," he said wearily. "I can't leave you tied up all night." He reached behind her and freed her wrists. Dinah brought her hands down beside her and lay still.

"I have to go back to the airport," she whispered plaintively.

"Sleep for a few hours, and I'll go with you. Please."

Dinah sighed. "All right. You win too."

He helped her remove the coat and sweatshirt, tossed them onto the floor, then hooked his thumb into her panties. "Won't feel right, if you keep these on," he explained. "Wouldn't be typical."

She almost smiled at his blarney. "You're right."

He drew the panties off her body and sent them flying across the room. Dinah guided him onto his back and molded herself to his side, her head on his big shoulder and her fingers buried in his chest hair.

"We'll get through this," he murmured. He stroked her cheek with one finger. "I'll always be beside you, taking care of you."

Dinah swallowed hard. She already knew how she intended to handle things back in Mount Pleasant, but she wouldn't upset the peaceful mood by telling Rucker right now. "No more talk for tonight," she urged. "I know you have a lot of thinking to do about what I told you."

"The hard part's done, Dee. You've told me what I've wanted to know all this time, and now I can help make things better."

"I've never talked to anyone but you about this."

"Feel relieved now?"

"Yes," she admitted slowly, nodding. "It was easier to discuss than I thought it would be." She paused. "I wish I'd had the nerve to tell you a long time ago."

"Sssh. Everything'll be fine, hon. You've got me. What else could you need?"

Nothing will be fine, she told him silently. But I trust you, and that's all I'm going to think about right now. She cried again, silently and more from relief than anything else, and he murmured gruff reassurances to her. Eventually, without ever uttering a word, they began to stroke each other in tender, slow ways. The caresses became so intimate that Dinah couldn't resist any longer. They both needed comfort.

She eased herself onto his thighs and took him inside her body, then made love to him with delicate movements and featherlight hands, showing that she cherished him and wouldn't be satisfied until she gave him intense pleasure. She refused to rush even when he began shifting under her, his neck and chest arched up, his head tilted back into the thick pillow.

After a minute he cried out hoarsely and curved himself up to her, a bow pulled taut by the special bond of passion and devotion they shared. Dinah grasped his sides and urged him to rise farther into the harbor of her body. He did, and she gloried in the sweet, deep sensation of being completely filled. Breathing raggedly, he sank back on the mattress as her hands moved over his face and torso, stroking him toward sleep.

He started to speak, but she placed her fingertip against his mouth, then shook her head. He nodded. Dinah brushed her finger lightly across his mustache, then touched each of his eyelids. They closed, and she caressed the drawn, swollen skin under them until she felt the small muscles relax in sleep. Dinah remained where she was for a long time, listening to him breathe, drawing the backs of her fingers across his temples, skimming his chest with reverent caresses.

When he woke up a few hours later, she was gone.

Ten

The furnace at Twittle County High decided to break down around ten A.M., and at noon the principal recessed school for the day. Dinah drove to city hall and went straight to her office, hoping for sanctuary. Todd Norins had stayed busy. After barging into her office yesterday, he and his cameraman roamed around town, telling residents about their mayor's criminal past and filming the responses. Today she'd been all too aware of the covert stares of students and teachers. They're not quite ready to start asking me questions, but that won't last long, she noted.

Dinah slumped over a strong cup of coffee at her desk, her eyes gritty from lack of sleep and her nerves frayed. She kept wondering how Rucker had reacted when he woke up alone. Not happily, she assumed. Lula Belle buzzed the intercom a minute later. "Do you know a feisty little blond woman named Millie Surprise?" Lula Belle asked.

Dinah stared at the phone console in disbelief for a moment. "Send her in."

Dinah heard the quick tapping of energetic feet on the linoleum of the hall floor. Millie, bundled in a rugged looking sheepskin coat that made her look like a small, blond eskimo, burst into the office.

"Rucker sent me!" she exclaimed. "He called and said you got the last plane out of Dallas before fog shut the airport down. I'm supposed to look after you until he

gets here. Dinah, he is fit to be tied! You shouldn't
have taken off like that!"

Dinah looked up at her, dumbfounded. Then she
muttered under her breath, "*He's* fit to be tied. I'll tell
you about being tied." Millie studied her with a puzzled
expression, and Dinah made a "nevermind" gesture.
"Does he think I'm helpless?"

"Oh, no, certainly not! But I'm trained in martial
arts"—she pulled a small pistol from her coat pocket—
"and I'm a skilled marksman—marksperson, from my
Navy days, you see."

Dinah gasped in alarm. Even Rucker's secretary was
a Clint Eastwood type. "Put that thing away! I don't
need help. I'm going to take care of this alone."

"Rucker said you'd feel that way. I'm supposed to
ignore you." She tucked the pistol in a big pocket in
the skirt of the black shirtwaist dress she wore, hung
her coat on a rack behind the door, shut the door
firmly, and plopped down in a chair across from Dinah. "Now, what's happened this morning? You look
very tired. But terrific, as usual. Tall women. I envy
you all. I love that red suit on you. Red's a power color,
you know."

Dinah was overwhelmed and just stared at her for a
moment. "Well," she managed finally, "what's happened,
you ask? Word is getting around. I walked in the teachers' lounge this morning and people practically cringed
with discomfort. They obviously didn't know what to
say, so they didn't say anything."

The intercom buzzed. "Dinah." Lula Belle's high-
pitched voice sounded worried. "There are four reporters in the lobby. Two television, two newspaper. They're
from Birmingham."

"Want me to go browbeat them?" Millie whispered
eagerly.

"No, no," Dinah murmured. She closed her eyes a
moment, gathering strength. "Lula Belle, tell them I'll
make a statement in two hours. On the steps out front.
I won't see anyone until then."

The door opened suddenly and Walter Higgins started

in. Millie leapt up and blocked his way. "Off limits!" she barked. "Move it or lose it!"

Dinah stood quickly. "Millie, this is a councilman."

"Oh." She sat back down, looking disappointed.

Walter came in and shut the door, eyeing Millie warily all the time. Then he turned his attention to Dinah, and his gaze became sympathetic. "I thought I'd better get your story firsthand. You know what kind of rumors circulate in a small town."

Dinah smiled thinly, her heart sinking. She nodded. "No, I had nothing to do with the disappearance of Jimmy Hoffa. I was just a kid when Watergate was going on, so I'm innocent on that count. And you'll never pin the Iran-Contra scheme on me."

Walter sat down in a chair next to Millie's. He tried to look relaxed and casual, but Dinah saw the concern underneath. He did his best *Dragnet* voice. "Just the facts, ma'am. Just the facts."

Dinah took a sip of coffee and straightened her shoulders. Rucker, I need you, she thought desperately. Then she shoved the wistful thought away and looked at Walter with calm eyes. "Now the fun begins," she told him.

The sky was a deep blue broken by high, scudding white clouds. The breeze was exceptionally cold for December. Standing on the steps in front of the city hall building, Dinah pulled her white wool coat around her for both physical warmth and emotional security. A crowd of townsfolk was gathering behind the reporters. Millie stood off to one side, her hands shoved in her coat pockets, her shrewd eyes sweeping the crowd as if she were daring anyone to make trouble.

So far, the reporters' questions had been no worse than she'd expected. They mainly wanted to confirm what was quickly becoming common knowledge. After dropping out of the Miss America pageant, she'd served a year in prison. Her father had been up for indictment on a number of felony offenses involving twenty-five million dollars, five million of which were still missing. As Dinah answered the inquiries she wondered bitterly which person or persons in town had called the press. She felt betrayed.

A man from *The Birmingham Sentinel* called out, "What are your plans for the future, Mayor Sheridan? Any books or movie deals under discussion? Are you going to pose for *Playboy*?"

Suddenly she'd had all she could stand of the television lights, the indelicate questions, the scrutiny. "I'm still considering my options," she answered. Actually, she was ninety-nine percent certain of her plans, but she wasn't ready to say so. "That's all I'm prepared to discuss right now. Thank you, and good day."

She started down the steps, aching with the cold and determined not to show how depressed she felt. A sharp voice cracked out, halting her. "Heah, now! I got somethin' to say to Madam Mayor and you press folks! I used to be mayor of this heah town!" Dinah felt repulsion settle in her stomach as portly, red-faced Mervin Flortney pushed his way through the growing crowd of spectators.

He wore a quilted khaki jacket over an excessively packed blue suit. His graying red hair waved wildly in the breeze. All Dinah could think of was a description she'd heard Rucker use for an arrogant maitre d' in a chic restaurant. Pompous, pig-lipped duck wart. It didn't make much sense, but it had just the right flavor to it.

"Heah!" Mervin said again. He waved a sheaf of papers as he came up the steps toward her. Millie started over, but Dinah shook her head. Mervin, owner of the Flourtney Plaza shopping center, drew himself up in an outraged-good-citizen stance beside her. "These here are recall petitions! I'm puttin' them in every bizness in town. We're not gonna have a thief for a mayor!"

Incredulous, Dinah took a step back, one hand rising to her throat in an involuntary gesture of distress. "You're entitled to start a recall drive," she told Mervin. "But don't you dare slander me!" This is revenge for my water main investigation, Dinah noted silently.

"And let me tell you another thing!" he blustered on,

"we're not gonna put up with a mayor who parades an immoral attitude in front of our children!"

"*What*?" Dinah gasped.

"Besides bein' a convicted criminal, this woman used to model lingerie and skimpy swimsuits!"

Dinah groaned. "Mervin, check your Sears catalog from eight years ago. It's not exactly a racy publication."

"And Madam Mayor voted herself the biggest pay raise in the history of Mount Pleasant!"

"Why, yes, Mervin. And now that I make fifty-five dollars a month instead of forty-nine, I'm buying the yacht I've always wanted."

"This woman cohabitates regularly with a divorced man!"

That was too much. "Mervin, don't be a total fool."

"Can't deny it, can you?" he taunted. "Oh, yes. Everyone knows that your fancy-dandy writer boyfriend comes up here all the time and stays overnight at your house! *Stays overnight* there!"

Out of the corner of her eye, Dinah blankly noted the arrival of a black Cadillac at the curb. Rucker? If the underlying issue of her public image weren't so at stake already, and if Mervin weren't taking himself so seriously, Dinah would have dismissed his ridiculous tirade without a flutter. But the combination of strained emotions and exhaustion was too much. She stared at the Cadillac, desperately searching for a response to Mervin's ludicrous insinuations, but her mind went blank. She was intensely aware of cameras clicking and whirring.

"See!" Mervin said gleefully. "You're ashamed of yourself, and it shows!"

Rucker bolted out of his car, his worried eyes already turning toward her. He ran up to the crowd, his trench coat falling open to reveal charcoal-gray trousers and a pullover sweater in shades of dusky blue. He got his colors right, Dinah thought numbly. He didn't always. I'm so proud of him.

"And what's more," Mervin yelled, "this woman is a liberal! A *liberal*!"

Dinah watched Rucker's eyes shift from her to Mervin. Under the mustache his mouth flattened into a grim line. "Mervin," she warned under her breath, "you're asking for trouble."

"Our mayor is a convicted criminal! A sex model! And a . . . a loose woman!"

Dinah winced. Rucker started pushing through the crowd, and now the look in his eyes was lethal. He shoved past a cameraman and charged up the steps, his fists clenched. When Mervin saw him, his red face lost most of its color. Dinah grabbed the front of Mervin's coat and shook him desperately.

"Mervin," she said as calmly as she could, "you'd better run like hell."

Mervin started backing up the steps. Dinah got in front of him just as Rucker grabbed for Mervin's lapels. "No, Rucker, no!" she begged in a tense whisper. "We're on camera!" She braced her hands against Rucker's chest and held him back. Rucker had eyes and hands only for Mervin, and he reached over her shoulders and got hold of Mervin anyway.

"Nobody talks about her the way you did," Rucker informed him in a rough voice. "You pompous, pig-lipped, son of a—"

"Rucker!"

Dinah was sandwiched between them, and all she could think was, ten to one odds, this was going to make the national news. "Rucker, please!" Mervin was flailing at Rucker's hands and hitting Dinah in the head in the process.

"I'm not gonna punch him, Dee, but I'm sure as hell gonna rattle his marbles!"

"This isn't a wrestling match, Rucker!"

"Boss, boss, cool out, man, cool out." Millie was involved now, clutching Rucker's right arm and tugging furiously. And then Dewey was beside them all, one huge dark hand anchored on Rucker's shoulder, the other wound in Mervin's coat.

"Break it up, boys," he instructed smoothly, "or you'll be sharing a cell." Rucker shoved Mervin and let him go. Dewey guided Mervin further up the steps and held him there like a fat puppy caught by the scruff of the neck.

"You'll pay for that, McClure!" Mervin yelled. "I'll press charges!"

"I'll press your head between a wall and my fist!" Rucker threatened back. "You keep your foul mouth shut about Dee!"

Dinah nearly groaned out loud. She clutched Rucker's arm with an unyielding grip. "Millie, help me push Godzilla inside the building!"

"I'll go peacefully," Rucker retorted.

"Good! It'll be the first peaceful thing you've ever done!"

He glared at Mervin and pointed a warning finger at him on the way into the lobby but didn't say anything else. Once inside, Dinah let go of his arm and turned toward Lula Belle, who was standing transfixed by the reception window where people came to pay their utility bills.

"I'm going to my office," Dinah told her in a fierce, formal voice. "I'm not taking any calls from anyone except the council. I'm not seeing any visitors."

All two hundred fifty pounds of Lula Belle quivered with determination under the green corduroy jumper she wore. "I'll see to it," she promised sternly. "Nobody's gonna get past Lula Belle Mitchum."

"Dee?" Rucker implored. "What about me?"

She twisted around and looked up at him with tearful eyes. "Are you *trying* to make me front-page news?" she asked in a desperate, angry voice. "You couldn't do a better job if you'd planned it!"

"I was protectin' you. Tryin' to protect you."

"I know that. I love you for doing it. You—" Her control dissolved and she pressed both hands to her face. "You brawling redneck!" He reached for her, but she shrugged his hands away.

"Dee, I—dammit, I didn't think about the press bein' out there. I overreacted."

"You always overreact!" She hurried down the hallway toward her office. "Just let me handle this mess on my own!"

"I'll be waitin' at your house for you, hon!" she heard him call as she slammed the office door.

The evening sky was fading into rose and amethyst over the pine grove that backed her neat little house. Dinah shut the station wagon's door and moved slowly across the yard, her shoulders aching with the day's strain. Rucker ran out of the house to meet her, wearing his best, most cheerful smile under worried eyes. He'd reverted to type by donning ancient jeans, a faded college sweatshirt, and jogging shoes.

"Hi," he said tentatively.

"Hi."

They walked the rest of the way inside without speaking. Pine logs crackled in the fireplace and the aroma of beef stew wafted deliciously through the air. Nureyev screeched from the kitchen and Jethro stared at her unemotionally, as was standard for him, from his bed of old towels in one corner of a wing-backed chair.

"No talk until I say so," Rucker commanded. "I want to know everything that happened after you went in your office, but not until I've got you fixed up."

When Rucker finished with his interpretation of *fixed up*, she was propped on the couch, wearing a shimmering blue kimono he'd bought her and sipping a glass of wine. He sat down and took her bare feet in his lap. He began to massage them, and the feel of his supple, caring fingers made Dinah sigh in appreciation.

"I wish I could bottle the effect your hands have on me. I'd carry it with me everywhere."

"Hmmm. Rub a woman's tootsies, she gets all fluttery. Pretty simple." His voice was cautious and low. "All right. Talk, ladybug. What happened?"

Her hand trembling, she set her wine glass down on the coffee table beside the couch. "Have a lot of people called here today?"

"Yep. I let your answering machine handle them. I was tryin' to write. Not very successfully, but tryin'. I kept worryin' about you."

"The board of education has called a special meeting scheduled for the day after the *USA Personal* story airs. They'll review the details." She laughed without humor. "And decide if they want a notorious woman for a history teacher."

"Dee, don't say—"

"I'm meeting with the city council the day after that. A closed session." She paused, her eyes hooded with fatigue, but amused. "Neada Gwynn at the tattoo parlor is on my side, at least. She told Lula Belle that I could have a free tattoo any time I want it."

They shared a bittersweet look. "There's a lot to be said for a free tattoo," he joked, his tone grim. He was quiet for a moment, his eyes troubled. "Still mad at me?"

When she stared down at her hands and didn't answer, he knew that she was. Rucker sighed. "Don't be so melodramatic. Your life is doin' fine. You've got me, right? And now you can stop running."

"I wasn't running. I was rebuilding."

"You were running." He waved one hand to emphasize his words. "Afraid to tell me about your past, afraid to tell anyone about your past, hiding in this hayseed town . . ."

"I love this town." Her voice faltered. "I—I thought you'd come to love it too."

"I do. But I don't think it ought to be the focus of your life. You've been hidin' here, no doubt about it."

She began to get charged up again, and her voice rose. "I was very happy, hiding here."

"And you'll be even happier now that you don't *have* to hide. You," he said sternly, "can do anything you want, if you're not afraid to try."

"I'm not afraid. But I have pride, and I'm not going to parade myself for public ridicule."

"You have too much pride."

"And you have a rose-colored view of the world, Rucker."

He got up, his eyes fierce. "I know how ugly the world can be. You have to remember how I grew up. But I also have faith in people."

Dinah stared up at him, her face flushed. "You think I'm a coward. Admit it." He hesitated, searching for a tactful retreat, and she read the truth before he could hide it. Dinah got up gracefully, her back rigid. "I see," she said icily.

He frowned deeply. "I just don't think you want to turn tail and hide anymore."

"Stop saying *hide*! Just because I don't subscribe to your folksy, naive, damn-the-torpedoes-and-full-speed-ahead philosophy—"

"My redneck philosophy, is what you mean," he said grimly, insulted. Dinah didn't answer, and now it was his turn to read the truth in silence. His expression became a mask of controlled anger. "I believe I'll take a drive." He went to the stand by the door and got his old aviator's jacket, then jabbed his arms into the sleeves. He was mad, and every brusque movement of his body illustrated that. "I'll cruise around town and do a little informal survey on the goodness of humanity."

"You'll be disappointed."

He slammed the door on his way out.

The night *USA Personal* aired was torment. Dinah sat on the edge of the couch, her back ruler-straight and her hands clasped tightly in her lap as she watched Todd Norins parade her story in front of a national audience. Rucker lounged beside her, brooding and quiet.

Afterward they turned the television off and sat gazing into the fire. Finally he touched her shoulder with his fingertips and said hoarsely, "You'll never forgive me for helping that man find you." Then he got up and went to the bedroom. Dinah followed him, her chest aching with sorrow because a part of her admitted that he was right, that his mistake would always be between them. Without turning on the light, he undressed down to his T-shirt and briefs, then got into bed and turned his back to her. Misery radiated from him.

Dinah suddenly felt more sorry for him than for herself. She stripped bare and got into bed with him, then curved herself to his broad back, nuzzled his neck, and wound her arm over his waist. "I can't sleep with a man who isn't naked," she teased gently. "I've become fond of your unclothed bohunkus."

He chuckled wearily. "You got it, then." He shucked his shirt and briefs, jauntily threw them across the room, and turned to face her.

"Come here," she urged, and reached for him. They lay on their sides, in each other's arms, their legs entwined. "I love you so much," he murmured, the words an apology for all that had happened.

"And I love you," she answered. "Sssh. We'll be all right." He rolled her onto her back and lay on top of her. Dinah wrapped her legs around him and looked up into the shadowed unhappiness of his face. "Oh, Rucker, you feel so good against me." Her voice was raspy with emotion and growing desire. "Make everything all right again. Please."

The intensity of the last few days spilled over into the night, and they both shivered. He ground his hips into the dampness between her legs, and she felt him stiffening. Dinah pulled his head to hers and kissed him deeply, teasing him with quick, desperate movements of her tongue.

Rucker trailed greedy kisses to her ear and said hoarsely, "No matter what happens, we'll always belong together."

Her voice was breathless. "Yes."

She stroked the tight, flexing muscles of his back and hips. He arched his body and entered her in a quick, almost desperate movement that made her cry out with pleasure. They held each other snuggly and chased the sadness away with a sudden wildness that tore restraint apart.

Dinah twisted and rose under him, responding to the fierce, possessive strength of his arms and the tormented way his fingers dug into her back as he lunged against her. Her cry of release drove him to thrust harder. He buried his head beside hers on the pillow, and she whispered encouragement to him as he moved faster.

He raised his mouth to hers and kissed her hard. She felt every muscle in his body contract with pleasure. Her mouth muffled his long, groaning sigh. The kiss continued in a series that slowly moved down her throat, until finally Rucker braced himself on one arm and dipped his head to nibble her breasts. Then he nestled his head next to hers again, sank one hand into her tangled hair, and guided her face into the hollow of his neck.

Dinah licked the hot, damp skin there. "Don't move," she whispered. "I want to fall asleep just like this."

"I'll hold you until you do," he promised, his voice languid and gruff. "I'll be right here. I'll be beside you when you wake up in the morning." He paused. "I'll be with you the rest of your life, if you want me."

Dinah caught her breath. A sweet feeling of confidence filled her. "I want you," she answered.

The kitchen was a haven of warm light against the cold, dark morning pressing against the bay window. Dinah padded in, preoccupied with tucking the tail of a pleated white blouse into a full black skirt that swung gracefully around her stockinged legs. "You're up awfully early," she murmured to Rucker. They shared a kiss as she went past him.

"Couldn't sleep. Decided to feed the critters."

He sat at the round kitchen table with a plate in front of him, tearing raw bacon into tiny pieces. Jethro clung to the lap of his white, terry-cloth robe and stared hopefully at the bacon. Nureyev hopped back and forth on his perch by the window, cocking his head as he eyed the bacon too.

"*Bonjour!*" he called. "*Sprechen sie* grits." He whistled a few notes that sounded vaguely like the opening bars of "Dixie," then launched into a garbled quote from Sartre.

"Grits," Dinah repeated dryly. " 'Dixie.' " She got a mug and filled it with strong coffee from a percolator on the counter. "Rucker, my crow is culturally confused because of you."

He chuckled, but the sound was more troubled than cheerful. She sat down across from him and sipped her coffee. "Rucker," she said in a rebuking voice. "Stop worrying about me. You have to go to New York. You've been scheduled to make this trip for two months. Your book editor is expecting you. The New York Press Club is expecting you. It's too important to postpone. You have to go."

"I'll be back in two days."

"That's right. Just two days."

"You're supposed to meet with the board of education and the city council while I'm gone. That's what worries me."

She smiled with a great deal more reassurance than she felt. "It's all going to be very calm and polite." He nodded then shrugged as if he were rebuking himself for being overprotective. It won't be difficult at all, she added silently. All I have to do is turn in my resignations.

Eleven

Dinah was seated at the piano practicing when the phone rang in the kitchen. Thinking that it was Rucker, she ran to answer it. But Lula Belle's voice leapt out at her over the receiver.

"Dinah, I think you better turn your TV to *Entertainment Tonight*. They just said something about Rucker being arrested in New York on account of he assaulted Todd Norins."

This isn't happening, Dinah thought desperately as she ran back to the living room and switched on the television. She knelt in front of her set, her hands clasped to her chest. A commercial was playing. Her breath short, she watched unblinking as the show returned. The beautiful blond hostess sent a grand smile into Dinah's living room.

"In New York, today," the smiling blonde said, "an altercation between award winning investigative reporter Todd Norins of *USA Personal* and best-selling author Rucker McClure ended with Norins unconscious on the floor of Napoleon's, a super-elegant Manhattan eatery."

Dinah gasped out loud. Beside the smiling blonde a publicity picture of Todd Norins appeared on the screen. "It seems that McClure took exception to an exposé Norins did last week on former Miss Georgia Dinah Sheridan. McClure, who is reputed to be the ex-beauty queen's boyfriend, cornered Norins in the restaurant.

Fellow diners said the two men exchanged heated words that ended when Norins threw a water glass at McClure. According to reports, McClure then grabbed the unsuspecting newsman by the coat collar, dragged him to a nearby table, and shoved his face into a plate of raw oysters.

Norins retaliated by tossing a punch at McClure, but the punch missed and hit a bystander"—the smiling blonde paused for effect—"who happened to be the owner of the raw oysters. In retaliation, that man hit Norins in the face, knocking him unconscious."

The blonde paused again, smiling broader. "Norins was treated and released at a Manhattan hospital. McClure and the unidentified oyster lover were arrested for assault and battery but were released on bond late today by New York City police. Charges and counter-charges are being filed by all three parties involved in the incident." She winked. "There's no word yet on the fate of the oysters."

"Rucker, how could you?" Dinah asked aloud, shaking her fists at the television. Anguish and fury combined to make her clutch her overwrought stomach as a wave of nausea hit her. Right before he left, he'd promised to behave. *Promised.* A few minutes later she was in the car, on her way to the airport and then to New York.

The high-rise hotel room was quiet and dimly lit, but the shadows seemed to hum with tension. Rucker stood at a big window gazing out at the cold rain slicing down on the Manhattan nightscape. He had his arms crossed over his chest and his long legs braced defiantly. He had stood this way ever since Dinah's angry arrival ten minutes earlier. His gray dress shirt missed the top five buttons where he had fiercely jerked the collar open, his gray trousers were wrinkled, and his auburn hair showed all the times he had run a hand through it.

"I did not," he repeated grimly, "do anything wrong. I was peaceful until circumstances called for me to defend myself."

Behind him Dinah continued to pace, her hands on the hips of the blue jogging suit she'd been wearing when Lula Belle called about *Entertainment Tonight*. She hadn't taken time to change. "You pushed the man's face into a plate of oysters, Rucker! That's not self-defense! You didn't have to touch him! How many more times is my name going to be mentioned on national television because of you?"

"I guess it'd be damned rude to expect you to thank me for what I did today." His drawling voice was furious. "To thank me for lovin' you so much that I couldn't let Norins walk into that restaurant and walk out again without tellin' him off on your behalf?"

"I love you! I love being protected! But not humiliated! What *did* you say to him?"

"I said—well—basically I said that he had the morals of a piranha. Just stuff like that. Just the truth."

"What particular remark made him throw the glass at you?"

"I believe it had to do with his hairpiece."

Dinah stopped pacing long enough to stare in shock at Rucker's back. "His hairpiece?"

"Yeah. He had one on today, and it was a real stinker. I said . . . hmmm . . . basically that when he got even fatter and balder than he is now, I hoped the network kicked his—kicked him into a toilet, where he belongs. That's when he threw the glass. He's a vain bastard."

"And your editor was the one with the raw oysters. The one who slugged Norins in the face?"

"Yeah. Larry." He paused. "Good old Larry. Didn't know he had it in him. See, though? I never hit Norins. I kept my promise to you."

Dinah knew then that she was defeated. Rucker was proud of what he'd done. Worse yet, deep down *she* was proud of what he'd done. She had never loved him so much or been so angry with him as she was right now. He wouldn't ever truly be repentant for his aggressive ways. He wouldn't ever stop trying to avenge her honor and his own guilt. She slumped into a chair and rested her forehead in her hands. It took a second to collect herself for the miserable words she spoke next.

"I think," she told him hoarsely, "that we shouldn't see each other anymore, until everything calms down."

"*What*?" She glanced up. He turned away from the window to gaze at her in utter disbelief. "Are you saying we should break up?"

"I'm saying that we need to go separate ways for a little . . . while. I can't bear the thought of more publicity like the kind I had today." She struggled to continue, her voice breaking. "You'll never change, Rucker. You'll always act first and think later. I'm just the opposite. I've thought . . . everything out."

She looked up at him. He was hurt, stunned, and mad. All of that showed in his fierce expression and the stance of his body. A muscle flexed rhythmically in his jaw. "And what other conclusion have you come to?" he asked in a low, strained voice. "That you don't love me anymore?"

Dinah shook her head slowly, her eyes rebuking him for speaking such nonsense. "Don't Rucker. This is killing me. I'll always love you. But I want to be alone until I get my life straightened out again."

"And just when will that be?" He took a step forward, his hands out in supplication.

Dinah took a deep breath. "When I move back to Atlanta. In about a month. I'll work until the end of fall quarter—"

"Have you resigned from your job?" The rising fury in his voice frightened her.

"Yes. And I've told the city council that I'm resigning as mayor also. Effective at the end of this month."

"No! No, ma'am, you're not goin' to run anymore!"

She stood, trembling all over. "It's done," she said grimly. "Done, Rucker. I won't change my mind."

"You most certainly will change your mind! I've never heard such crap in my life! I'm ashamed of you!"

She gasped. "And I'm ashamed of you!"

Those awful words hung between them like a double-edged knife, cutting both ways. "Damn your time," he said in a barely audible voice, his hands clenching and unclenching. "If that's the way you feel, then go ahead and run. Run from everything. Run from everybody who cares about you, includin' me. Go ahead. I won't try to stop you anymore."

Dinah nodded, her throat on fire, all her despair clotting into a thick knot inside her chest. "I've been hurt too much in the past. Maybe I am running. But it's the only way I know to protect myself."

"It's not the right way."

"Try to understand. Please."

"I won't ever understand."

"Then . . . I suppose I'd better just leave." He didn't say anything, and she retrieved her purse and coat from the bed. "I'll call you."

"Do what you want."

"I'm going now."

"Fine." He threw one hand out in a gesture of dismissal, and his eyes were cold.

Stunned, Dinah went to the door. Despite everything they'd said just now, she prayed for the slightest yielding, the slightest indication on his part that he wanted her to stay, to talk, to work it all out somehow. The signal never came.

"Good-bye," she finally managed, just mouthing the words because her voice was gone. He turned back toward the window and stood with his head lowered, his hands on his hips. His shoulders flexed harshly as he struggled to take deep breaths. He was still standing there, sorrow tearing him apart, when she left.

It was a sad excuse for a Christmas tree, but it suited her mood precisely. Dinah sat on the couch and looked grimly at the stunted, lopsided pine tree she'd bought from the Kiwanis's tree lot. Even decorated in beautiful white lights and the fine old ornaments that she'd kept from a prized collection of her mother's, it was ugly. Jethro was asleep on the carpet under it, and Nureyev was perched on one of the stronger branches. He kept pecking a crystal reindeer ornament as if he expected it to turn, miraculously, into something edible.

"I like you anyway," she told the tree. "You're mine, and I like you."

The sound of cars pulling up her graveled driveway made her get to her feet anxiously and go to the front door. Dinah switched on the porch light and gazed out at a half-dozen assorted vans, pickup trucks, and cars that were vying for parking space alongside her station wagon. "What in the world?" she said aloud. It's a lynch mob, she thought sarcastically.

But familiar people, including students, fellow teachers, Walter, Dewey—wearing street clothes instead of his uniform—and Lula Belle, climbed out of the vehicles. They bore bags and cardboard boxes, and they started singing "Rudolph the Red-Nosed Reindeer" as they made their way up the porch steps. Blinking in shock, Dinah opened the frame door and watched them through the screen of the outer door. They came to a stop on the porch and sang to her loudly, off key, and with great cheer.

"How do," Walter said when they finished. "We came to have a party. Saturday night is a fine time for a Christmas party, don't you reckon, Mayor?"

"I reckon," she answered blankly.

"Then open your screen door and step aside."

She did as he directed and they marched past her, smiling and nodding their individual hellos. Within minutes they'd converted her kitchen table into a party center, complete with punch bowl and an array of food. Lula Belle went to the baby grand in the living room and began pounding out "God Rest Ye Merry Gentlemen."

Dinah took a cup of punch from Dewey and sat down weakly on the hearth. When Lula Belle finished playing, Walter called for a toast. "To our fine mayor," he said solemnly, "who doesn't know how much we need her."

Dinah ducked her head and fought back tears. "Thank you. Thank you all. The past week has been . . . fantastic." She'd gotten supportive cards and letters from nearly everyone in town. Her students had deluged her with small presents, mostly food and handmade Christmas ornaments. She'd hung the ornaments proudly among her mother's finery on the bedraggled little tree.

"I have a poem for you, Miss Sheridan." Dinah raised her eyes to find Dewey's eight-year-old daughter, Lucille, gazing at her with nervous brown eyes.

"A poem for me?" Dinah gave her a wide, encouraging smile. "Let me hear it!"

Lucille held up a piece of notebook paper and began to read: "She works hard and never stops, looking out for our homes and shops, teaching history in our school, living by the golden rule, smiling out at everyone, with pretty eyes all full of fun. We wish she'd stay and never go, and all because we love her so."

"The rhyme's a little funky," Dewey noted, "but the spirit's right."

Dinah wrapped Lucille in a hug that made the startled little girl squeak with surprise. "It's beautiful," Dinah told her fervently. "The best." Lucille was grinning when Dinah let go of her. Her grin slowly faded.

"What's wrong?" she asked, studying Dinah's face. "I made you cry!"

Dinah hurriedly brushed the tears off her cheeks. "I'm crying because I'm happy! I'm so happy that you all feel the way you do. . . . You're magnificent . . ." She got up and headed toward the hallway. "I'm so . . . happy . . ."

"So happy that she's got to go powder her nose!" Lula Belle interjected tactfully. "Go on, Dinah. We'll crank out some more Christmas songs on the piano until you come back."

"Thank you. This is really wonderful." Dinah hurried to her bedroom and shut the door. "Happy," she whispered hoarsely, leaning against it, tears streaming down her face. "Oh, Rucker, you were right about them. Oh, Rucker, I miss you."

• • •

The next day, Sunday, she called his house repeatedly but got no answer. More people dropped by, just out doing their pre-Christmas visiting, they said as they politely admired her ugly tree and plied her with gifts. By the end of the day she had six fruitcakes, four dozen Christmas cookies, two bottles of liquor, and a stack of coupons good at local businesses courtesy of Wally Oscar and the Chamber of Commerce. This is a conspiracy, Dinah thought. And I've never felt so honored in my life.

But then evening came, the visitors left, and depression settled in again. Dinah called Rucker's house one more time, got no answer, and wearily went into the living room to grade papers. A clock ticked loudly from its place on the bookshelves. The fire popped and sizzled. Stillness and silence enveloped her as she sat cross-legged on the couch, her briefcase on her knees. Dinah read one essay, stared into the fire for a long time, read another essay, stared into the fire for another long period, then finally set the briefcase on the floor and stared into the fire full-time.

She heard a car pull into the driveway. More fruitcakes, she thought, but was glad for the diversion. Dinah went to the bathroom to check her hair and makeup. When she came back the visitor was rapping firmly on her door. The visitor was Rucker.

Her heart rate uneven, Dinah opened the door and gazed at him with an expression that she knew held desperate happiness. He looked magnificent in a leather jacket, jeans, and a bulky red sweater, but he would have been a welcome sight even in the grubbiest of his grubby old clothes. He was the dearest sight she'd ever seen, no matter what. And he looked back at her with a greedy attention to detail that exceeded her own.

"I brought you the best Christmas present I could find," he finally said. "She's out in the car."

Dinah raised one hand in a questioning gesture as he turned and walked out to the Cadillac. Bewildered, she squinted into the edge of the porch light as he opened the passenger door and helped a gray-haired woman out. She wore a full-length fur coat and she carried herself with a dignity that spoke of wealth and prestige. Her eyes flew to Dinah immediately then away just as quickly, as if she were very nervous.

Rucker held the woman's arm as they walked into the house. She offered a tentative smile as Dinah took the fur and Rucker's jacket. When she returned from placing them on her bed, the visitor was seated on the couch and Rucker had settled on the hearth. Dinah sat down on the couch and glanced from him to his guest. She was petite and beautifully dressed in a tailored gray suit. A thick strand of pearls adorned her burgundy blouse, and her hands bore diamond rings that caught the firelight. She crossed one fine-boned hand over the other and shifted uncomfortably.

Rucker cleared his throat. "Dee, I want you to meet Mrs. Franklin. Mrs. Franklin, this is Dee—Dinah Sheridan." Dinah held out a hand. Mrs. Franklin shook it, her eyes rising to Dinah's in anxious acceptance.

Then she said in a shaky voice, "We met once before, years ago, at a party my brother gave at his home in Atlanta."

"Your brother," Dinah echoed blankly, searching for a memory.

"Donald Beaumont," Mrs. Franklin supplied.

Dinah slowly sat forward on the couch, her pulse skipping. "Of course. My father's senior vice president. Uncle Beau."

Mrs. Franklin nodded, and her lower lip trembled. She looked down at her hands, her throat working spasmodically. "Go on," Rucker told her gently. "Tell her."

"My brother," she said after a moment, "was the man who embezzled the money."

Dinah was dimly aware of the room closing in on her. She put a hand over her parted lips and shut her eyes, feeling as if she might sway dizzily. "You okay, Dee?" Rucker's concerned voice brought her back to control.

She nodded vaguely and looked at Mrs. Franklin. "Is this a joke?" Dinah whispered.

"N-no, oh, no."

"Rucker, is this a joke?"

"No, Dee. Sssh. Listen to Mrs. Franklin."

"Don . . . had some alcohol problems. He was a good man, at heart . . . had been a very good man. But he had these problems, you see. . . ." Mrs. Franklin began to cry softly. "Did you know that he drank too much?"

Dinah frowned, trying to think and having difficulty. "Yes. He and my father were friends for years. They served in the Army together. They went to college together. I grew up calling him Uncle Beau. When he died a few years ago, I went to his funeral. But I didn't know he was . . . an alcoholic."

"He was. There were drugs too. But your father stood by him. You have to understand that your father wanted to save him from the awful mistake he'd made."

"My father was trying to undo the embezzlement? *Uncle Beau* took the money? Are you certain?"

Mrs. Franklin nodded, still crying. "Your father arranged an early retirement for him. Then he tried to clean up the mess Don had made. Don came out to California to live with my family. He was in a very bad way. . . . We hospitalized him for months."

"*He* took the money?" Dinah knew she sounded foolish by repeating the question, but the enormity of Mrs. Franklin's words kept them from registering. She looked to Rucker for help. "How did you decide to talk to . . ." She pointed lamely to Mrs. Franklin.

"I've been huntin' for answers," he told her. "Ever since New York. I . . . uh . . . needed something positive to do. So I dusted off my old reporting skills and started nosin' around. Mrs. Franklin was just one of my leads. The right one, as it turned out. She was ready to help."

"Ready to confess!" Mrs. Franklin interjected tearfully. She sat forward on the couch, her hands bunched in her lap. She gazed at Dinah with wretched apology. "After your father died in that horrible plane crash, I thought . . . it's finished. No one can be hurt now. I never knew that you were implicated in the investigation. I never knew about your trial . . . or I would have come forward to help you. I swear I would! But I . . . I thought that the issue was closed and that, by remaining silent, I could make certain that my brother lived out his last years quietly, without scandal."

She shook her head at Dinah. "But I knew how wrong I had been when I heard about you in the news recently. And that awful story on USA Personal. I realized that I'd made an unforgivable mistake by not revealing my brother's crime. I didn't kn-know what to do. . . ."

"But when I called her, she came through like a champ," Rucker said. Dinah realized suddenly that he'd relied on all his easygoing charm to coax this terrified creature into the open.

She felt Mrs. Franklin's tear-stained eyes on her, and met them. The frail hand reached out to her. "I'm so sorry that you're suffering again on Don's behalf! I'll make it right! I'll tell everything to the authorities! To the bank . . ."

"What about the rest of the money?" Dinah asked, her voice raspy. She didn't know what she felt at this moment. Happiness? The story hadn't had time to produce happiness yet. Anger? Yes. "My father died!" she said tersely. "He was innocent, and he died from a careless flying error caused by being distracted and worried! And it was all because of your damned brother!" Mrs. Franklin bent double and sobbed into her skirt. Rucker rose quickly but looked uncertain as to which of them needed soothing the worst. "Where's the rest of the money!" Dinah demanded.

"In . . . in an account in Switzerl-land!" Mrs. Franklin cried. "Your father was trying to move all the embezzled f-funds back w-where they b-belonged. He h-had a plan! But when he died I d-didn't know how to return the part I knew about! So I j-just left it there!"

"And how did embezzled money end up in my savings account?"

"Don put it there! He was so . . . irresponsible. He told m-me it was a secret g-gift for you because h-he liked you! I thought no one would ever trace where the money came from!"

"How foolish can you be!"

"Dee, go easy, go easy on her," Rucker urged. He patted Mrs. Franklin's shoulder then sat down between them. Dinah kept staring at Mrs. Franklin and vaguely felt Rucker clasp her hand tightly in his.

"Go easy on her? I'm sorry, but th-this is too much! I've spent y-years—" now Dinah heard her own voice begin to sound like Mrs. Franklin's "—y-years despising my f-father . . . my father . . . because I didn't know . . ." Dinah put her free hand over her face. "Oh, Daddy, forgive me!"

Rucker took her in his arms then and rocked her gently. "Now we're gettin' somewhere." He kissed her forehead. "Let go, Dee, let go."

"I'll make it all right!" Mrs. Franklin murmured pathetically. "I'm so s-sorry!"

Remorse compelled Dinah to pull away from Rucker and vault to her feet. He grabbed at her hand, obviously thinking that she was bent on violence. She stepped past him and put her arms around Mrs. Franklin's pitifully quivering shoulders. Instinct, some need to heal and be healed, was the guiding force.

"I'm trying to understand, I really am," she whispered raggedly. "I know what happened wasn't your fault. I know I'm hurting you."

Dinah sank down to her knees and Mrs. Franklin's arms went around her. "Poor dear," Mrs. Franklin sobbed against her shoulder. "I'll make it right, I swear."

"You already have. You've . . . given me my father back." Dinah gazed tearfully over Mrs. Franklin's head at Rucker. He leaned back on the couch, his expression drawn tight with control, his eyes riveted on her. She mouthed the words *I love you dearly* to him. He nodded but didn't offer the pledge in return. The pain of that subtle rejection made Dinah close her eyes and bow her head close to Mrs. Franklin's, thinking wretchedly, I've got everything now. Everything except what I need most.

• • •

When Mrs. Franklin was bundled in her fur again and seated in his car for the return trip to the city, Rucker came back in the house to get his jacket. Dinah presented it to him in worried silence, her eyes locked on his face. He looked down at her with a guarded expression.

"I'm going to stay in Mount Pleasant," she said desperately. "I'm not . . . running. I'd already decided that, before you came here tonight."

He showed no reaction. His voice was low and casual. "What made you change your mind?"

"Faith. I got my faith in people back. They"—she waved a hand to indicate the townspeople—"have been wonderful to me. They don't want me to go."

"I'm glad, Dee."

She stared up at him, her heart racing. "Is that all?"

His jaw worked for a moment, and he frowned. "For right now, that's all."

"Rucker?" she said fearfully. "I—"

"You're real grateful to me right now," he interrupted. "But bein' grateful isn't the same as . . ." He struggled for a moment then cleared his throat. "It isn't enough. Maybe after the grateful feelin' wears off, you'll remember that you're ashamed of me and my methods."

"No," she said hoarsely. "I'm not ashamed. Please. I wish I'd never said that."

"I'll always do things that embarrass you, Dee. I'll always act first and think later."

"I can live with that."

He almost smiled, but the anguish inside him weighed the effort down. "Can you? I want to believe that, I really do. Stay here, think on it, make sure. I don't want to hurt you anymore—"

"And I don't want to hurt you!"

He bent forward and brushed his mouth across hers in a quick, restrained kiss. She sank both hands in his sweater and tried to keep him from pulling back. "No, Dee, no." He grabbed her hands and gently pulled them away. "I want you to think on it."

"I don't want to think!"

A hint of his old humor crooked one corner of his mouth up in a wry smile. "You always want to think. People with high IQ's are like that."

"But Rucker—"

"Good night," he whispered, and kissed her forehead. She reached for him again, but he stepped back, his chest rising with a harsh breath. "Don't . . . I want you to be sure."

After a second she regained her dignity. Her chin came up. "All right. I'll stay here and think."

He smiled at her authoritative tone. "You do that, possum queen."

She watched him walk to the car. I'll show you, Mr. McClure, she thought. I'll find some way to prove that I love you just the way you are.

Twelve

"Somebody call a paramedic. McClure is sick."

Rucker lowered his poker hand and stared balefully at the men who circled the table. "What are you gripin' at now?" he asked.

Bill Harte, a Methodist minister affectionately known to Rucker's readers as the Reverend Snooker Hornswaggle, propped his chin on one hand and glared back. "The card you just gave up was the ace of diamonds, friend."

"Oh." Rucker shrugged. "Well, pardon me."

Richard McClansky, who always appeared in Rucker's column as Ed Howe of the accounting firm Dewey, Cheatum, and Howe, snorted in disbelief. "Rucker Mc-Clure, poker addict, has no interest in the game. How many years have we been meeting here to play poker, boys?"

"Since the dawn of time," noted Silas Spencer, an Atlanta police detective who had successfully avoided a print persona so far.

"And have you ever seen His Royal Highness not pay attention to the game?"

"Hell, no," Richard answered. "Excuse me, Reverend Bill."

"Heck, no," Bill corrected coyly.

Rucker threw his cards down and slumped back in his chair. Jethro was asleep in his lap, and he stroked the possum's head distractedly. "Go on without me. I'm worthless tonight."

"Let's not confine that description to tonight," Silas added.

The doorbell chimed upstairs. Rucker got up wearily, set Jethro in the chair, and headed toward the door of the game room. "Take my cards," he told the group sardonically. "Take my money. Kiss my grits."

I don't give a damn about poker or anything else, he thought as he climbed the stairs. This is just another lousy night without Dee.

The bell chimed again before he got to the front door. "Hold your horses," he called. Probably some kid sellin' Christmas cookies, Rucker decided. *Bah, humbug.* He jerked the door open and froze, staring at the apparition that stood there. "Dee?" he said in shock.

She ran a hand over her tall, beehive hairdo. "Not Dee. Deedee." She winked at him and stepped inside, lugging a huge, wicker picnic basket. "Ooooh," she crooned in a cutesy voice, "I'm so happy to see you." She kissed him on the cheek and wrinkled her nose at him playfully. "I'm from Acme Rent-a-Cheerleader. See?"

She turned around, exhibiting a tight gold sweater with a large M sewn on the bosom and a pleated, gold-and-black cheerleader's skirt. A very short cheerleader's skirt that allowed ruffled gold panties to peak out when she moved. She was two inches taller than usual because of the black, stiletto-heeled shoes she wore. They had little black ankle straps. She touched the M on her chest. "M for McClure," she said sweetly. Then she giggled. "I'm on your team. I'm all yours."

He was dumbfounded. She kissed his cheek again. "Follow me," she ordered in the same flirty voice as before. "Are your poker buddies here? Oh, I just *love* taking care of your friends! Let's go downstairs and see them!"

"Uh, uh . . ." he tried.

"Now you just hush, you big sweet boy. I have all sorts of wonderful food in this basket." She handed it to him and fluttered her eyelashes. "You're so big and strong. You carry it for me, pleeeease."

She pranced down the hallway, putting every possible wiggle into the walk. "Come along, now, honey bunchkins. My chicken is getting cold."

"Dee! What the hell!"

"Ooooh, I *love* it when you talk masterfully!"

She disappeared down the stairs to the game room, and he hurried after her, his mouth permanently open in shock. By the time he reached the bottom step, she was cooing over Bill, tweeking Richard's cheek, and smiling at Silas. They'd met her a time or two before and they were in shock over the transformation. Rucker set the picnic basket on a bar in one corner of the room. She sidled over to it.

"Now you sweet boys just come over here and eat all you want," she ordered cheerfully as she began removing huge containers of food. "I made fried chicken with extra lard, gooey potato salad, buttery biscuits, and—ooooh!—chocolate cupcakes with raisins and sprinkles on top! My honey bunny's favorite meal."

By now, everyone but Rucker was convulsing in laughter. "Hot damn!" Silas chortled. "Excuse me, Reverend Bill."

"Hot durn!" Bill agreed.

"Dee?" Rucker said plaintively, looking bewildered. "Dee?"

"*Deedee*," she coaxed, her hand on one hip. "Now you just sit down and I'll bring you a plate, sweetie pie. Can I get you a beer?"

"I'll get my own," he mumbled, and hurriedly did so. He sat down in his chair and watched her with incredulous eyes as she arranged food on a paper plate and wiggled over to him with it balanced on one hand, waitress style. She put it down on the table in front of him, pulled a plastic fork and a napkin out of the waistband of her skirt, and handed them to him with a flourish.

"And after you eat, I'll do all the cleaning up," she cooed. "I just want you to sit there and enjoy your game. You work so hard. You deserve to play."

He looked down at the food, then back up at her. "Enough! Just hold on! Hold everything!" He stood up and snatched her hand in his. "We've got to talk!"

"Ooooh, I *love* it when you take charge!" She trailed after him, back upstairs. He tugged her into the living room and pointed to the couch.

"Sit!"

She didn't sit, she lounged, her long, gorgeous legs stretched out invitingly on the cushions. She gave him a coy, come-hither look and crooked one finger at him. "You sit, too, big guy."

"I'll stand." He put his hands on his hips and angled one leg out to the side. "What is this all about?"

"This is about compatibility. I'm showing you that I can be exactly what you want."

"I want you just the way you are—were!"

"You want me?" She twirled a finger in the edge of her beehive. "I want you, too, you *darling* good old boy. You lovely, brawling, redneck."

He held up his hands. "You don't have to say that."

"I'm not just saying that!" She got up, her facade gone and her blue eyes very serious. "I want you just the way you are too. The way you always have been. Generous, caring, sensitive, unpredictable, wild—"

"Uh, we'll be going now," Silas said from the door. Bill and Richard stood behind him, grinning foolishly and holding plates of food. "We can see that we're not—uh—needed."

They turned and exited quickly, and a few seconds later the front door shut behind them. Rucker sat down on the hearth, his eyes still on Dinah. "Dee," he said, "I'll always be rowdy. Always."

She nodded and knelt in front of him. "And I'll always love you for it. I may not always approve, but I'll always love you. I'm inordinately proud of you, you know."

"You are?"

She nodded again and grasped his face between her hands. "How can I not be proud of a man who tries to whack people on my behalf? How can I not love a man who puts love ahead of common sense?"

After a silent moment in which he looked desperately into her eyes, he grabbed her in a bear hug. They tumbled to the floor together, their legs tangled, and he ended up lying half on top of her. "My hair, my hair!" she protested in mock dismay. "You're scaring the bees!"

"Run, bees, run." He sank both hands in the brunette bubble and kissed her roughly. Dinah sighed in delight and opened her mouth to encourage the intimate sweep of his tongue.

"Hmmmm." She kissed him back with matching excitement, her hands moving wantonly over his back and hips. "I need you," she whispered between more kisses. "I had to find some outrageous way to make you want me again."

"I've never stopped wanting you." His eyes full of devotion, he looked down at her. "But I wanted you to want me without bein' embarrassed."

"Oh, Rucker," she said gently, "I'd rather be embarrassed with you than be dignified with any other man in the world."

He laughed then, his eyes glistening and his expression so full of delight that she felt like crying with relief. "I've missed your laughter," she told him. "And your voice." Her tone became throaty. "And your touch."

His laughter faded, replaced by a quiet, intense gaze that held a lifetime's worth of promises. "I'll give you a new supply."

"Right now?" she asked in a soft, breathless voice.

He got up, pulling her to her feet alongside him. Then he swooped her up in his arms. His eyes burned into her and his voice was gruff. "Right now, Deedee."

There was something delightfully ridiculous about being in bed naked with Rucker, a picnic basket, and a possum. Dinah held a chicken leg up to Rucker's mouth and he groaned. "No more," he begged. "I can't budge."

"You were budging quite well an hour ago," she teased softly. "Quite well."

He smiled at her and slid his arm closer around her shoulders. "Inspiration. That's the key."

Dinah tossed the chicken leg. It landed neatly on a paper plate at the foot of the bed. "Two points," she noted jauntily. Jethro was stretched out on his side, nearby, snoring. "I didn't know that possums snored."

"Our baby is special." Rucker let go of her long enough to push himself down to the edge of the bed and gather the limp little animal in one hand. He slid back up and settled comfortably on the pillows, with Jethro on his stomach. "Look at him. He didn't even wake up." He held out one arm so that Dinah could snuggle close to his side again.

She put her head on his shoulder and stroked Jethro's side. "How can you tell? He looks like this all the time."

Rucker put his hand over hers, and she lifted her face to look at him quizzically. They were silent for a moment, smiling at each other. "Dee," he said slowly, "this possum needs a last name. He needs to be legitimate. He needs his mother around all the time." Tears came to her eyes because she suspected what he was going to say next. "Will you make him respectable, hon? Will you marry me?"

She nodded, her throat tight. "I can't let Jethro go any longer without respectability.

"Oh, you're a noble mother," he whispered. They kissed tenderly, and afterwards he nestled his face into her lopsided hair. "I'm suffocatin'," he teased after a moment.

"I'll go brush my hair out right now."

"Nah. I'll do it for you. In a little while." His arm tightened around her. "Let's just stay still."

"Good idea," she murmured. She thought for a minute. "How are we going to live together, Rucker? With me in Mount Pleasant and you . . ."

"I'm movin' to Mount Pleasant."

She raised her head and looked at him in shock. "You want to come back to small-town life?"

"Uh-huh. It suits me, don't you think? I can write my column and my books from any place. I ain't a big-city boy. I'm a good old boy. I belong in the hills where I can hunt and fish."

"You don't hunt or fish."

"Well . . . I'll find something to keep me busy in my spare time." He smiled rakishly at her. "I'll make babies."

"You will, will you? I believe I have some small part in that process."

"Yeah, but I'll have to take care of them a lot after they're born 'cause you'll be governor."

"Governor!" She smiled wryly. "Governor Deedee Mc-Clure. Has a nice ring to it, doesn't it?"

He looked pleased. "And I'll be First Lady."

Dinah looked at him askance for a moment. Then she nodded and kissed him again, her eyes shining with adoration. "I suspect," she whispered, "that the state is in for a wonderful adventure."

THE EDITOR'S CORNER

June is certainly a month for gorgeous, passionate, independent, loving, tender, daring, remarkable heroines! With three of the six women of the month being redheads, you can be sure to expect fireworks! Magdelena is washed right into her lover's arms in the rapids; Lux falls into her lover's arms with a giant teddy bear; Meghan has risky plans for her man; Candace finally wants to give all; Lacey's free spirit needs taming; and Randy learns to surrender . . . All this and a whole lot more in our June LOVESWEPTs. Read on to learn about each book and the wonderful heroes who fall in love with these six fabulous heroines.

In **CONFLICT OF INTEREST** by Margie McDonnell, LOVESWEPT #258, Magdelena Dailey, our heroine with long, wild hair, is rescued from a Colorado river by Joshua Wade who steals a passionate kiss as his reward. Joshua is a sweet seducer, a man made for love. Magdelena needs quite a bit of convincing before she changes her plans and lets a man into her life again, and Joshua is up to the challenge. There's no resisting his strong arms and tender smile, and soon Magdelena is riding the rapids of love!

Lux Sherwood is a raven-haired beauty in **WARM FUZZIES**, LOVESWEPT #259, by one of our perennial favorites, Joan Elliott Pickart. All Lux needs is one of her very own creations—a giant teddy bear—to get Patrick "Acer" Mullaney's attention. Acer is a star quarterback with a serious injury that's keeping him out of the game—the game of football, that is. He's definitely strong enough to participate in the game of love, and here's just a taste of what Acer has to say to Lux:

> "My needs run in a different direction. I need to kiss you, hold you, touch you. I need to make love to you until I'm too exhausted to move. I don't want to be just your friend, Lux. I won't be."

(continued)

What's a woman to say to such a declaration? Lux finds the right words, and the right actions in **WARM FUZZIES**!

We're so pleased to bring you our next LOVESWEPT for the month, **DIVINE DESIGN**, #260, by first novelist Mary Kay McComas. With a redheaded heroine like Meghan Shay and her daring scheme, we're certain that Mary Kay McComas is headed for LOVESWEPT success! Her hero in **DIVINE DESIGN** isn't bad either! Who can resist a long, tall Texan whose eyes gleam with intelligence *and* naked desire. Michael Ramsey has all the qualifications that Meghan is looking for—in fact he's too perfect, too good looking, too kind, too wonderful—and she can't help but fall in love, and that's not part of Meghan's plans. Ah, the best laid plans . . .

Barbara Boswell delivers another moving love story with **BABY, BABY,** LOVESWEPT #261. By popular demand, Barbara brings you Candace "Barracuda" Flynn's love story. And what a love story it is! Candace wants a second chance with Nick Torcia, but Nick is wary—as well he should be. Candace burned him once, and he isn't coming back for more. But something has changed. Precious new babies have brought them both an understanding of love. Still, Nick needs to lay the past to rest. Here's a sample of the intensity of their encounter:

"Why did you lead me on, Candy?" Nick demanded, his onyx eyes burning into hers.

"Not for revenge," she whispered.

"Then why, Candy?"

Her heart seemed to stop beating. He was so close to her, close enough for her to feel the heat emanating from his hard, masculine frame.

"Nick." His name escaped from her throat in a husky whisper, and she tried to move closer. Desire, sharp as a stiletto, sliced through her. She wanted to lose herself in his arms, to feel his hot, hard mouth take hers. She gazed at him with undisguised yearning.

But Nick wouldn't let her close the gap between them. He held her wrists, controlling her movements and keeping her anchored in place. "Tell me, Candy."

Tyler Winter is the man who tames Lacey Lee Wilcox's free spirit in **FOR THE LOVE OF LACEY**, LOVESWEPT #262, by Sandra Chastain. Tyler is a renaissance man—an artist, businessman, and an absolutely irresistible hunk! Is

(continued)

he a flirt or really a man Lacey can trust her heart to? Tyler showers her with kisses, gives her wildflowers, and takes her on picnics, but still Lacey is afraid of losing her heart. With just a little more convincing our heroine loses her fears and listens to her heart:

"Tyler, turn me loose," Lacey ordered.

"Nope," he said, moving his mouth toward hers.

Not again, she begged silently. Too late. She was being kissed, thoroughly kissed, and there was no way to stop him. Tyler finally drew back and grinned down at her with undisguised joy.

"Tyler," she protested, "you don't know what you're doing."

"You're right, and it's been a long time since ignorance felt so good. Kiss me, Lacey."

In **HAWK O'TOOLE'S HOSTAGE** by Sandra Brown, LOVESWEPT #263, Randy Price can't believe what's happening to her. It's 1987, yet she's just been abducted by a masked man on a horse! No, this is not part of the old west show she was watching with her son. Who is this masked man? And why does he want Randy? Hawk O'Toole is an Indian Chief with very good and honorable reasons for kidnapping Randy Price, but he doesn't plan on the intense attraction he feels toward her. She's his hostage, but fate turns the tables, and he becomes her slave. Love has a way of quieting the fiercest battles as Randy and Hawk find out.

Happy Reading! Remember to look for The Hometown Hunk Contest next month—it's your big chance to find the perfect LOVESWEPT hero!

Sincerely,

Kate Hartson

Kate Hartson
 Editor

LOVESWEPT
Bantam Books.
666 Fifth Avenue
New York, NY 10103

ENTER
THE DELANEYS, THE UNTAMED YEARS
MISSISSIPPI QUEEN RIVERBOAT CRUISE
SWEEPSTAKES
WIN
7 NIGHTS ABOARD THE LUXURIOUS
MISSISSIPPI QUEEN STEAMBOAT
including double occupancy accommodations,
meals and fabulous entertainment for two

She's elegant. Regal. Alive with music and moonlight. You'll find a Jacuzzi, gym, sauna, movie theatre, gift shop, library, beauty salon and multi-tiered sun deck aboard...plus a splendid dining room and lounges, beveled mirrors, polished brass, a Grand Saloon where big band sounds soothe your soul and set your feet to dancing! For further information and/or reservations on the Mississippi Queen and Delta Queen Steamboats CALL 1-800-458-6789!

Sweepstakes travel arrangements by
RELIABLE TRAVEL INTERNATIONAL, INC.

Whether you're travelling for business, romance or adventure, you're a winner with Reliable Travel International!
CALL TOLL FREE FOR INFORMATION AND RESERVATIONS
1-800-645-6504 Ext. 413

MISSISSIPPI QUEEN RIVERBOAT CRUISE SWEEPSTAKES RULES AND ENTRY FORMS ALSO APPEAR IN THE FOLLOWING BANTAM LOVESWEPT NOVELS:

THE GRAND FINALE **MAN FROM HALF MOON BAY**
HOLD ON TIGHT **OUTLAW DEREK**
*CONFLICT OF INTEREST ***DIVINE DESIGN**
*WARM FUZZIES ***BABY, BABY**
*FOR LOVE OF LACEY ***HAWK O'TOOLE'S HOSTAGE**

and in

THE DELANEYS, THE UNTAMED YEARS:
COPPER FIRE; WILD SILVER; GOLDEN FLAMES

*On sale week of May 2, 1988   SW'10

OFFICIAL DELANEYS, THE UNTAMED YEARS
MISSISSIPPI QUEEN˙ RIVERBOAT CRUISE
SWEEPSTAKES RULES

1. **NO PURCHASE NECESSARY.** Enter by completing the Official Entry Form below (or print your name, address, date of birth and telephone number on a plain 3" x 5" card) and send to:

> Bantam Books
> Delaneys, THE UNTAMED YEARS Sweepstakes
> Dept. HBG
> 666 Fifth Avenue
> New York, NY 10103

2. One Grand Prize will be awarded. There will be no prize substitutions or cash equivalents permitted. Grand Prize is a 7-night riverboat cruise for two on the luxury steamboat, The Mississippi Queen. Double occupancy accommodations, meals and on-board entertainment included. Round trip airfare provided by Reliable Travel International, Inc. (Estimated retail value $5,500.00. Exact value depends on actual point of departure.)

3. All entries must be postmarked and received by Bantam Books no later than August 1, 1988. The winner, chosen by random drawing, will be announced and notified by November 30, 1988. Trip must be completed by December 31, 1989, and is subject to space availability determined by Delta Queen Steamboat Company, and airline space availability determined by Reliable Travel International. If the Grand Prize winner is under 21 years of age on August 1, 1988, he/she must be accompanied by a parent or guardian. Taxes on the prize are the sole responsibility of the winner. Odds of winning depend on the number of completed entries received. Enter as often as you wish, but each entry must be mailed separately. Bantam Books is not responsible for lost, misdirected or incomplete entries.

4. The sweepstakes is open to residents of the U.S. and Canada, except the Province of Quebec, and is void where prohibited by law. If the winner is a Canadian he/she will be required to correctly answer a skill question in order to receive the prize. All federal, state and local regulations apply. Employees of Reliable Travel International, The Delta Queen Steamboat Co., and Bantam, Doubleday, Dell Publishing Group, Inc., their subsidiary and affiliates, and their immediate families are ineligible to enter.

5. The winner may be required to submit an Affidavit of Eligibility and Promotional Release supplied by Bantam Books. The winner's name and likeness may be used for publicity purposes without additional compensation.

6. For an extra copy of the Official Rules and Entry Form, send a self-addressed stamped envelope (Washington and Vermont Residents need not affix postage) by June 15, 1988 to:

> Bantam Books
> Delaneys, THE UNTAMED YEARS Sweepstakes
> Dept. HBG
> 666 Fifth Avenue
> New York, NY 10103

- -

OFFICIAL ENTRY FORM
DELANEYS, THE UNTAMED YEARS
MISSISSIPPI QUEEN˙ RIVERBOAT CRUISE SWEEPSTAKES

Name _____

Address _____

City _____ State _____ Zip Code _____